Something was nuzzling her ear.

Alison smiled and tilted her head up, sniffing the air to test it. It smelled good. Male.

Wriggling closer, she found herself enveloped in a sensual kiss. Of the toe-curling variety. Warm lips covered hers. Strong hands at her back drew her close. Their tongues entwined, and Alison moaned.

She undulated a little closer, trying to fill in every possible gap of space between them. Then, in the twilight of half sleep, she felt her hand hit something completely unfamiliar—at least in her experience. Her hand latched on to what felt like a tiny foot.

Baby Felicity let out an indignant howl.

Alison bolted upright—and found herself straddling Ross's body.

His *very aroused* body.

ABOUT THE AUTHOR

The author of numerous historical, contemporary and young adult romances, Liz Ireland makes her home in Texas, where she loves to swim, read and care for a houseful of pets. Ever since she can remember, Liz has been a fan of movies, a passion she indulges at every opportunity.

Books by Liz Ireland

HARLEQUIN AMERICAN ROMANCE

639—HEAVEN SENT HUSBAND
683—THE GROOM FORGETS

HARLEQUIN LOVE & LAUGHTER

59—THE HIJACKED BRIDE

HARLEQUIN HISTORICALS

286—CECILIA AND THE STRANGER
330—MILLIE AND THE FUGITIVE
410—PRIM AND IMPROPER

Baby for Hire

LIZ IRELAND

TORONTO • NEW YORK • LONDON
AMSTERDAM • PARIS • SYDNEY • HAMBURG
STOCKHOLM • ATHENS • TOKYO • MILAN • MADRID
PRAGUE • WARSAW • BUDAPEST • AUCKLAND

To Joyce, for helping my granny read these books.
A million thanks aren't enough!

ISBN 0-373-16767-9

BABY FOR HIRE

This edition published by arrangement with Harlequin Books S.A.

Printed in U.S.A.

Chapter One

She was on the run from a nun.

Alison Bennett hit the door to the reception room for Little Angels Modeling Agency like a Thoroughbred bursting through the starting gate. Her receptionist, Dee Kirk, gasped by way of greeting as Alison raced for her office. "You weren't supposed to be back till next week!"

Avoiding explanations, Alison waved but kept speeding ahead. The waiting area was always a sea of little kids and the stern or doting faces of their parents, but today she saw the hopeful hoard only in a blur. Maybe if she whizzed by fast enough, no one would notice she was wearing an ill-fitting nun's habit or that she was being tailed by a sister in sneakers.

She didn't dare look back, for fear that Sister Joan would gain on her. But when Alison finally reached what she considered the safety of her office, the nun was right on her heels, with baby Felicity's stroller parked in front of her.

"Goodness!" the deceptively diminutive nun exclaimed, not the least bit winded from keeping up with Alison's frantic pace. "You certainly seem in a hurry to get back to work!"

That was the understatement of the century.

Before being convinced by Sister Joan that she should spend a week at St. Felicity's convent "on a retreat," Alison had been strung out. Her business was booming, but she hadn't taken a real vacation in five years. The growing number of people seeking the services of Little Angels hadn't yet begun to match the burgeoning legion of hopefuls out in her waiting room every day; the pressure of having to turn children away was beginning to tell on her nerves. To make matters worse, her mother still called daily to ask if Alison was going to stay single for the rest of her life. As if her marital status was a sign of some kind of stubborn domestic ineptitude.

And, oh yes, this week marked the one-year anniversary of the day Alison was left standing at the altar by Mr. Wesley Westerbrook, an event her mother still blamed her for. That might have had something to do with her stress level.

She'd needed to get away, and at Sister Joan's urging, she'd packed her bags for a week at St. Felicity's, hoping the convent would provide just the peace and quiet she was seeking. She envisioned herself alone in a cozy bare room lit by a single glowing candle, with birds chirping outside her window as she reflected on the joys of solitude. She'd be a nun for a week, along the lines of Audrey Hepburn in *The Nun's Story.* There would be no phones, no crestfallen clients, no mother pestering her about having let Wes get away. And at the end of her time there, she would come out refreshed, spiritually cleansed....

So much for rosy expectations. Instead of a week of peace and quiet, she'd been treated to five days of

Catholic boot camp, and the commandant of the outfit was Sister Joan herself.

"Your retreat cured me of all my problems," Alison said. "Juggling the careers of a hundred pint-size models now seems like a cakewalk compared to what I've just been through."

She looked around at her large beige-carpeted office and could have cried for joy to see it again. How could she have ever taken such luxury for granted? How could she have thought that running a baby-modeling agency was exhausting? How could she have forgotten the hard lessons of twelve interminable years of Catholic school?

"Oh, come now," Sister Joan said, chuckling dismissively.

But it was the truth. Alison crossed her arms and cocked a no-nonsense brow at Sister Joan. "That convent of yours gives a whole new slant on the term slave labor. I toiled more in five days than I have in my entire life. And were my efforts even appreciated?"

Sister Joan shifted uncomfortably. "You can't blame Sister Catherine for being just a wee bit put out. You did chop down all her prized berry bushes."

"Well, how was I to know? They looked like weeds to me." Just the memory of the shame the mother superior of St. Felicity's, Sister Catherine, had made her feel for a few impulsive snips of the pruning shears caused Alison to shudder. She had to be the first person ever to wash out of convent camp.

"I guess St. Felicity's and I just don't mix."

"But you were so wonderful with the children!"

Alison groaned. The nursery at St. Felicity's—she would have nightmares about it for years to come!

That was where Sister Catherine had sent her after the gardening disaster. After all, Alison was used to handling kids professionally. But four days of pulling nursery duty at St. Felicity's day-care facility reminded her of how lucky she was to deal with children indirectly, while they were supervised by parents.

By the end of the week she didn't have an item of clothing that hadn't been finger-painted, ripped or puked on. Today, after darling little Felicity herself upchucked grape juice on one of Alison's favorite outfits, Alison was reduced to wearing one of Sister Joan's spare habits, a gray jumper and white shirt so small she now understood how boa constrictor victims must feel. To make matters worse, the skirt, one that fell modestly to Sister Joan's knees, hit Alison about midthigh, making her look less like a novice nun than a novice streetwalker.

She would be perfectly happy if she never had to face another baby again. Unfortunately most of her clients were ten and under. And the most disagreeable, uncontrollable one of all was sitting right in front of her, pouting imperiously.

Sister Joan tapped a Reebok-clad toe impatiently. In addition to jumpers and crisp white shirts, the sisters of St. Felicity wore modified veils and white stockings—but the footwear was apparently left to individual taste. In Sister Joan's case, sneakers were a wise choice. The woman definitely needed shoes that could keep up with her.

"So, Alison, do you think there will be any work for little Felicity this week?"

Alison looked down at Felicity's adorable mouth, still bearing a telltale purple ring from the grape-juice incident, and shook her head grimly. "No offense, Sister Joan, but I don't think Felicity will—"

"But she was wonderful in that diaper commercial. You said so yourself!"

Baby Felicity, a foundling left on St. Felicity's doorstep, had experienced one triumph in her short career: she had played a crying baby in a leaky diaper for a diaper commercial. It was a part she had realized to perfection. Unfortunately, when it came time for Felicity to play the happy baby in the dry diaper, she hadn't been able to stop crying. Another child had to be brought in for the happy baby.

Hard to believe, but in the kid-eat-kid world of children's modeling, an episode like that gave a baby a bad reputation. Felicity was known as a baby with an attitude. No one wanted to work with that kid.

"I'm sorry, Sister."

Sister Joan tried another tactic. Full-throttle guilt.

A long dramatic sigh issued from the nun's lips. "Maybe the day that poor little Felicity wouldn't stop crying she just happened to be remembering that she's all alone in the world, with no one on earth except a few impoverished nuns to help her."

Alison steeled herself. "But Sister Joan—"

"You wouldn't believe the amount of compliments we get on her, Alison. Ever since *D Magazine* ran that article on Felicity's appearing in the commercial, St. Felicity's donations have gone up thirty percent."

With those words, the hoped-for guilt crashed over Alison in a mighty wave. By not getting Felicity more work, Alison felt it was like taking bread out of the mouths of nuns and babies.

"Did I tell you she was almost adopted as a result of all the publicity?"

"How wonderful!"

"*Almost,*" the nun repeated. "The couple backed out."

Alison's heart sank. Felicity's being adopted might have been the answer to her prayers. If the child was in different hands, hands not quite so eager to have a fund-raising tot… But already Felicity's earnings had started a trust fund for orphaned children. And with the extra donations the convent had received from the article Felicity had appeared in, a picture-perfect child surrounded by beaming nuns, St. Felicity's had plans to break ground for a new day-care center. More money would be a help, of course….

Keeping Felicity out of work made Alison feel like the worst kind of heel and, in fact, caused her some anxiety. There was sure to be an unpleasant place in the hereafter for folks who deprived nuns and orphans of a healthy profit.

"But of course," Sister Joan went on, pretending not to notice Alison's discomfort, "some other family might want little Felicity—especially if they see her in an ad…"

Raised voices and a short scuffle in the reception area momentarily diverted their attention. A stage daddy and Dee were apparently having it out.

"Honestly!" Sister Joan muttered in disgust. "Some people are so pushy!"

No kidding. Sister Joan, for instance, was like a steamroller in a wimple.

Alison sighed, returning her attention to the immediate problem. "You know, work doesn't necessarily guarantee that people will find out who Felicity is and where she lives."

Sister Joan's eagle eyes focused sharply on Alison,

who became certain the nun knew as much about wheeling and dealing as Donald Trump. "No, but we've got an interview lined up with the *Morning News* next week. The *Morning News,*" she repeated for emphasis. "I doubt one of the largest dailies in the state will run an article about a baby model if they discover the baby's career has hit the skids!"

Alison shook her head regretfully. Nothing changed the fact that there was no work for Felicity today—even if she had had the temperament of a little angel along with the face of one.

Alison was just getting around to telling Sister Joan this unfortunate but undeniable fact when the growing ruckus out in the reception area escalated to a frenzy and exploded into her office. The door flew open and two people spilled inside. First came Dee, backward, as if she had been bodily blocking the threshold, followed by the tallest, handsomest, most arrogant-looking stage dad Alison had ever laid eyes on.

For a moment she could only ogle him. She remembered once before being this tongue-tied in a man's presence. When she'd met Wes. This man had the same air about him—the same careless arrogance.

"Are you in charge here?" the man asked in a deep commanding voice.

Alison folded her arms over her chest, hoping to cover the fact that she was having as hard a time catching her breath as Dee was. The man, with his dark reddish-blond hair and blue, blue eyes, was arresting, to say the least. He had the type of bronzed skin that seemed to result only from time spent at very exclusive tropical resorts. The fact that he had a body like a Greek god beneath that expensive suit of his didn't escape her notice, either.

But none of these intriguing details meant he had a right to barge in like he owned the place. "Yes, I'm in charge, but as you can see, I'm busy with another client," Alison said, attempting to keep the nervous quiver out of her voice and present a cool, detached, professional persona. "Now if you'll just wait out in the lobby with your child—"

The man shot her an imposing glance. "My name is Ross Templeton," he announced, as if this should mean something. "I have no child."

"Then I'm very sorry. This is strictly a *children's* agency. If you're looking for work—"

"I'm not a model," he interrupted again. "I'm a hotelier."

Alison blinked, finding her attention snagged on his handsome face. Hotelier? Actually he was a *hunk,* but that was beside the point. She swallowed. "Well, Mr. Templeton, if you're looking for a child to place in an ad, you've come to the right place. But right now—"

Again the high-handed man chopped her off in mid-sentence, as if his time was too precious for him to wait for complete thoughts to be expressed. "I see I'm not putting this clearly enough for you." His lips curled into a tight smile and he took a step toward her. Alison's breath hitched. The man filled the room with his presence. "I don't need a baby for a commercial. I just need it for the weekend."

She frowned. "Are you doing a promotion?"

A slight hesitation preceded his answer. "Not exactly."

Alison withheld a huff of exasperation. "Mr. Templeton," she said with waning patience, "this is a modeling agency, not a leasing service."

"I guess you could call this an acting job, then."

It sounded just plain strange to her. "You already said it wasn't a commercial. What kind of acting job do you have in mind?"

For the first time since barreling into her office, Templeton was hesitant to speak. "It's...a private matter."

Warning bells sounded in Alison's head. Despite the man's expensive clothes and imperious manner, he had to be a nutcase. *A private matter?* No way would she send one of her clients to this guy! She glanced at the others in the room to gauge their reactions. Sister Joan was sending the man a disapproving scowl, and Dee looked even more apologetic for allowing Mr. Templeton to bully his way into the back office.

Ross Templeton was also trying to see how his short explanation had gone over. Sensing certain rejection unless he stated his case more bluntly, he stepped forward and admitted, "Actually what I need is a baby to be my child."

HELL, HE SHOULD HAVE just gone to the mall, handed the first woman he saw with a baby a fistful of bills and rented one that way. But no, Ross thought with disgust, he'd assumed going through an agency would be easier, more professional. He was the type of man who liked things settled with contracts and signatures, not a shady exchange of money. He'd made a special trip to Dallas because he'd found this place in the Yellow Pages at his dad's house.

But now these people were staring at him as if he was a criminal! Of course, it didn't help that he was dealing with a bunch of nuns, which had surprised him at first. But it made sense. After all, the place was called Little Angels.

One of the nuns was a small older woman, with gray hair peeping out beneath the short white wimple on her head. The other nun, however—the one who appeared to be in charge—was like no nun he'd ever seen. Not that he'd been in contact with many. But this one was pretty—a real looker. She had thick shoulder-length brown hair, so dark and shiny it appeared almost black. Her skin was creamy, her heart-shaped face beautiful and her eyes big, brown, and lovely.

Right now those eyes gawked at him with a look approaching horror, he couldn't help thinking what a shame—why would a knockout like that become a nun?

Not that it mattered to him. He just needed a kid.

He dreaded having to confess the reason behind his need to rent a baby. Yet no matter how judgmental the nuns' gazes, they couldn't make him more uncomfortable than the disappointment in his father's eyes, looking up at him from a bed in an intensive-care unit, when the old man had announced he was dying.

"My only regret is that I'll never see a grandchild, Ross," Henry had said. "I always thought that, with as many wild oats as you were sowing, eventually you'd have to settle down some day."

"I did, Dad," Ross had explained. "I settled down and got to work."

"But not to the most important work," his father chastised him. "Family. No other job is as difficult—or rewarding."

Family. Ross scowled now, just thinking about it. He'd thought about having his own family once. With Cara. The memory brought forth a mental snort of derision. What a wonderful mom Ms. Career-first would have made! For that matter, he probably wasn't such hot parent material, either. Maybe renting *was* the way to go. He didn't hanker after domesticity like some men did. He'd always considered marriage and kids a trap.

Anyway, it was hard to think of any other family besides his father. Bringing in an impostor to pose as a grandchild was somewhat underhanded, yet it was only because of his devotion to his father that he was willing to attempt the charade. All his life he had striven to be a dutiful son. He couldn't bear the idea of the old man dying disappointed in him.

But apparently the younger nun was going to be an obstacle.

"Let me get this straight," she said after a few moments of stunned silence. "You want to *hire* a baby you can pass off as your son?"

He took in the disbelief in her brown eyes and smiled in spite of himself. "Or daughter," he clarified. "I'm not particular."

"Apparently not!" the woman he'd had such a tussle with in the reception area exclaimed. He couldn't help glancing at her several times, wondering how a girl with about ten earrings and a pierced eyebrow ended up in a place run by a religious organization. Maybe this was one of those liberal orders.

The younger nun eyed him skeptically. "I hate to even ask it, Mr. Templeton, but why? Why would a person want to do such a thing?"

Under normal circumstances Ross would have known just how to handle the woman in front of him. She was pretty, and the first moment their eyes had met, he thought he caught a glimmer of appreciation in hers. If she'd been any other woman, he could flirt with her until he'd persuaded her to do what he wanted—a technique he'd been honing since he'd learned the difference between little boys and little girls.

But a nun? He wasn't sure flirting was the right thing to do in this circumstance. It didn't help that this particular nun, although she might have renounced men and worldly things, definitely sent out mixed messages. She didn't appear entirely comfortable being a nun, for one thing. That habit, which looked perfectly respectable on her older counterpart, seemed almost indecent on the younger nun's curvy frame, especially the way her black pumps showed off her shapely legs. And she chose not to wear anything to cover her head, letting that gorgeous hair hang free; he'd never seen a nun wearing any makeup before, either.

Then again, she didn't exactly strike him as a cream puff. The rigid tough way she stood telegraphed to the world that she was all business. Only the slightest hint of weariness in her tack-sharp gaze and the memory of that mutual hitching of breaths when they'd first seen each other indicated she might be vulnerable to his appeal.

Ross decided to play the sentiment card. She *was* a woman, and most women were sentimental. That was their weakness.

He cleared his throat. "You see, I'm doing this for my father. He's had a heart attack and probably doesn't have long to live. He's very old and very dear to me, but I'm afraid in one respect I've disappointed him. He would die a happy man if he knew he had a grandchild."

As he spoke the words, the office seemed to grow

very still, very quiet. The gentle clicking of the second hand on the large desk clock was suddenly almost deafening. Ross began to feel self-conscious. Especially when the young nun merely stared at him with the same openly disapproving stare.

After what seemed like an eon, she spoke. "That's the craziest thing I've ever heard of."

So much for the sentimental approach. Ross suppressed a sigh. "Then you won't help me?"

She put her hands on her hips. "I should say not! Furthermore, I wish I could call the police."

"The police?"

"The ethics police, if there were such a thing," she said hotly. "You should be ashamed for even contemplating such a subterfuge!"

She might not look like a nun, but she sure sounded like one.

Ross took note of the other two women and felt a little buoyed up by their reactions. The older nun was dabbing her eyes with a snow-white handkerchief, and the receptionist was looking at him—almost swooning over him—as if he was a movie star.

"I'm willing to pay you a large amount of money," he said.

"I'll bet!" the dark-haired nun tossed back at him scornfully. "A man who would lie to his father like that *would* believe he could simply barge into an agency and rent a child."

"A *very large* amount of money," he clarified.

"You could give me the moon and it still wouldn't matter," she answered. "What you're planning is despicable!"

For some reason the venom in her voice stung more than it should have, causing him a rare moment of self-doubt. Was what he was doing really so terrible? He didn't think so. But he hadn't asked anyone else's opinion before he'd run off half-cocked to Dallas on this odd mission.

Not that it mattered. Once he settled on a plan of action, he rarely changed course. "Fine," he said. "I'm sure there's someone out there who wouldn't mind earning twenty thousand dollars."

A moment of stunned silence ensued. Then, before he could turn and walk away, a firm hand clamped down on his arm. It belonged to the older nun.

"Twenty thousand dollars?" the diminutive woman echoed in awe.

He nodded.

"Mr. Templeton," the senior nun announced, "you've got yourself a baby."

Ross grinned.

It was at that point he noticed a fourth set of eyes—the roundest bluest eyes he'd ever seen—peering up at him from a stroller. He'd been so preoccupied with the nuns that he hadn't noticed the baby in the room. The blue eyes were framed by an adorable baby face with soft peachy skin, glowing chubby cheeks, and feathery-fine brown hair. Even the pout on the little bow-shaped pink lips was positively adorable. In short, this had to be the cutest, sweetest, most picture-perfect little kid Ross had ever seen. He felt an instinctive coo building in his throat and just managed to swallow it back in time to avoid making a damn fool out of himself.

"It's *yours?*" he asked the nun doubtfully.

The younger nun stepped forward. "*She* is a foundling from St. Felicity's."

Good, Ross thought, quickly evaluating the advantages to this situation. *No parents to deal with.*

"We'd be happy for you to take her," the nun said, beaming at him.

"Sister Joan!" The other nun was aghast. "How can you even think about participating in such an undertaking? We don't know this man from Adam!"

"No, but you've probably stayed in a Templeton Inn at some point in your life," Ross said.

"You mean you're *that* Templeton?" the pierced receptionist said, clearly impressed.

Ross drew himself up, liking the receptionist more and more. He felt a moment of guilt for tackling her in the waiting area. "His son, actually."

"No wonder you can throw away twenty grand just to rent a baby!"

"We do *not* rent babies!" the younger nun cried, arms akimbo on shapely, gray-wool-clad hips.

"Why not?"

"Because what you're doing is...is..."

Bringing happiness to a dying man, Ross was about to say, but once again the older nun helped him out.

"He's just trying to bring his father a little happiness at the end," Sister Joan said. "Surely, Alison, you can't consider that a bad deed. Even Mother Superior won't—especially not after I explain about the twenty thousand dollars."

The other nun, Sister Alison, sputtered in dismay. "W-what he's doing is terrible!" she insisted. "It's lying!"

Sister Joan did seem to weigh her argument for a moment, then shook her head dismissively. "Just of the little white variety."

As the nuns debated ethics, Ross pulled out his

checkbook. Money seemed to be talking, which was fine with him. All three women looked up at the brisk sound of the check being ripped from his checkbook.

"I didn't know who to make it out to," he told Sister Joan as he handed it over.

She took the piece of paper and gazed at it reverently. "Ten thousand dollars!" Her voice was a hoarse whisper.

"The rest will be paid when the kid has completed its assignment." At Sister Alison's look of consternation, he corrected himself, tongue firmly in cheek. "Beg your pardon, *her* assignment."

"Wait just a minute!" Sister Alison cried.

The woman was beginning to annoy him. "What's the matter now?"

She scowled at him, then turned again to Sister Joan. "You can't just do this, can you?"

The nun blinked. "Oh, I think so. Like I said, I believe Sister Catherine will understand."

Sister Alison threw up her hands and rolled her eyes when she caught Ross trying to chuck the baby on her dimpled chin.

"Hello..." Ross glanced at Sister Joan. "What's her name?"

"Felicity."

"That's a mouthful for such a sweet little thing."

"Sweet!" Sister Alison practically howled the word, and then shot him a dark look as if to say, *You're welcome to her.* Something in the glance made Ross a bit anxious, and he drew back, inspecting the little girl once more. But no, she appeared as cute as a bug and sound as a bell. Just what he'd been looking for.

He straightened. "I'll expect Felicity at my hotel tonight at six-thirty sharp. We've got a long way to go."

"Go?" Sister Joan asked. "Go where?"

"To my father's ranch in West Texas. It's only a little over an hour by plane." He frowned. "The baby *can* fly, can't she?"

"Well, of course, but…"

He knew it was too good to be true.

The poor woman looked at him imploringly. "But I can't just let you simply *take* Felicity. Someone will have to go along with her, to look after her."

Hmm. Stupidly he hadn't thought about this, but of course she was right. "I could hire someone to go with her. A woman."

Sister Joan looked panicky. "I wouldn't feel right leaving her in the care of a stranger."

"But I would need a woman along, anyway," Ross said. "After all, my father might wonder where this baby came from."

Sister Alison smirked. "I'll bet."

Ross, deep in planning, ignored the sarcasm. "I need someone who can pose as the mother."

"Sister Joan, couldn't you go with the baby?" the receptionist asked.

Everyone jumped on the answer and turned to Sister Joan, but one look at the dour little woman in her nun's habit was enough to explain exactly why she couldn't go. She hardly fit the part of an unwed mother!

The woman herself shook her head, her expression subtly scandalized. "I don't think Sister Catherine would approve of that at all."

"I'll have to find someone," Ross said.

"Then you'll have to go bribe someone at an adult modeling agency," Sister Alison suggested. "Most of the clients here are from the Barney set."

Sister Joan put her foot down. "I will *not* send this child off with a strange woman. Someone I know and trust must go with her."

"But who?" the receptionist said.

Ross looked at the younger woman. Despite the earring problem, she was in her early twenties and pretty in that half-starved waif look so many kids went in for nowadays.

"Perfect!" Sister Joan cried.

Ross nodded. "You'll do fine."

"But I...I couldn't!" the receptionist protested. "I mean, like, I *really* couldn't. My sister's wedding is tomorrow and I'm maid of honor!"

Ross withheld a huff of dismay. Things weren't progressing as neatly as he had hoped.

He looked at Sister Alison. Absolutely not.

With his father's illness, his nerves were already stretched taut. A prickly disapproving nun on his hands wouldn't help matters. Especially when the nun had a face like an angel and a body like Raquel Welch, with shapely legs and the kind of curves a man just itched to wrap his arms around.

Not that she was his type. He usually went for lanky, athletic blondes. But as brunettes went...

Her eyes widened and he knew he'd been gawking like a teenager with hormones on overdrive—*at a nun!* Good heavens! He couldn't believe he would even be thinking of a woman of God as being a *type,* or whether he *went for* her or not.

He absolutely couldn't take Sister Alison...but what choice did that leave him? He didn't know the first thing about babies. And maybe her being a nun would have its advantages, putting her clearly off-limits. He didn't need any entanglements right now. The only thing he cared about was getting back to his father.

"I know!" The receptionist turned helpfully to Sister Alison. "Couldn't *you* go?"

As they all looked at her, the woman's eyes bugged in horror. In fact, she appeared to find the prospect far more distasteful than he did. "Absolutely not," she said adamantly.

Ross turned back to Sister Joan. "Wouldn't Sister Catherine disapprove of her going with me, too?"

Three puzzled glances met this question.

After a moment Sister Joan quickly stepped forward and took his arm. "No, no. Sister Catherine was just saying to me this morning that Alison should get out of the convent..."

"Good," he said decisively. Sister Alison was still shaking her head, but Ross was certain the twenty thousand dollars would make the mother superior bring Sister Alison to heel. "Meet me in the lobby of the Melrose tonight at six-thirty."

But he couldn't have his single mother looking like a nun. Although, even in her nun's habit, Sister Alison was strangely alluring.

Ross stopped dead in his tracks. *Alluring? A nun?* Now he *knew* the tension created by his father's illness was getting to him!

He turned back to Sister Alison and tried to ignore the sexy way her lips were puckered into a frown.

"Pack regular clothes for the trip," he instructed her. "Remember, you're supposed to be a normal person."

SISTER JOAN WAS in awe as Dee ushered Mr. Templeton out of the agency. "My, that man works fast!"

"Arrogance." Alison smirked. "He's taking a lot for granted."

The nun squinted at her suspiciously. "Shouldn't you be going home to pack?"

"Pack for what?"

Sister Joan blinked. "For your trip."

Alison shrugged. "I never said I was going anywhere," she said. "In fact, the last thing I said was absolutely not."

The nun's expression verged on the hysterical. "But you *must* go! The poor man's counting on you. His dear father..."

Alison sent her a level stare. "The man's richer than a Rockefeller, and his father would be better off without being lied to."

"But the twenty thousand dollars!"

Alison steeled herself against the coming guilt trip. "Why don't you go, Sister Joan?"

"But he didn't want me."

She inspected the nun's appearance. "Maybe if you'd been dressed differently... After all, the man assumed *I* was a nun—something you were perfectly willing to let him go on believing—so I don't know why we shouldn't be able to pass you off, in Mr. Templeton's words, as a normal person."

"You know that wouldn't work," Sister Joan insisted.

Alison didn't flinch. "I'm not going."

Sister Joan held out her hands imploringly. "When Sister Catherine hears what you've done for us, I'm sure she'll be grateful. Who knows? She might name the new building the Alison Bennett Day Care Center."

Alison took a deep breath. Sister Joan *would* keep harping on that subject! "I can't do it."

The tiny nun managed to look crestfallen and accusing all at once. "I see. Of course, you know the building may never be finished without Mr. Templeton's money...."

Ouch. "He can find someone else."

Sister Joan nodded. "Oh, yes. He might find another baby, even. We might not get the money at all."

"Sister Joan, please—"

"Never mind, Alison." Sister Joan shrugged, then went on mercilessly, "This might have been the last time I would ever have to trouble you about Felicity and trying to raise money."

"Stop!"

But she didn't stop. "As it is, you might be seeing very little of me, anyway. Once Sister Catherine learns that I had my hands on twenty thousand dollars and then lost it..." She looked down regretfully at the check and started to twist her hands as if she was about to tear it in two.

Alison picked up her purse. "All right!" she said, finally caving in to guilt.

The things she did for that convent!

Sister Joan beamed triumphantly. "It's all for a good cause."

"But I had plans for this weekend!"

Sister Joan was unimpressed. In fact, now that she

had gotten what she wanted, she looked as carefree as a kitten. "Now what could you possibly have to do that is more important than twenty thousand dollars?"

Alison's temperature rose about ten degrees. "For one thing, I was going to relax! After a week at St. Felicity's, I need a retreat from my retreat."

Sister Joan laughed, completely unfazed. "Well, then! This works out perfectly. You'll have a lovely relaxing weekend with Mr. Templeton."

Alison groaned. "With that overbearing man? He's so arrogant, just like all filthy-rich men. In fact, he's just like Wes—who, if you'll remember, is exactly the person I've been trying so hard to put out of my mind."

She didn't mention that she also found Ross Templeton even more wildly attractive than she had Wes, which was the most dangerous point of all, to her mind. She'd sworn off rich good-looking men a year ago. Unfortunately someone seemed to have forgotten to inform her hormones.

She sighed as she gathered up her things. There *was* a bright side to things, she realized. After this weekend, she would have banked up good deeds to spare.

She hitched her purse over her shoulder and headed for the door, breezing right past Sister Joan and her charge. "Bring the baby to my house later," she instructed, wanting to put off responsibility for the child as long as possible.

A weekend with little Felicity could be pure torture—she already had the wrecked wardrobe and frazzled nerves to prove it. Felicity might look the picture-perfect baby now, but if there was one thing Alison had learned from experience with that tyke, it was that the kid was great at auditions—and incredibly cranky when the pressure was on.

One thought at least made her smile. Ross Templeton didn't know just what kind of trouble his twenty thousand dollars was buying him.

Chapter Two

What did one pack to pretend to be a nun pretending to be a mommy?

Alison's closet was stuffed to the gills with clothes, but they all seemed to fall into one of two categories—business suits and very casual wear. A suit probably wouldn't be right for the performance she was being forced to give, yet on the other hand, she didn't want to present herself to Ross Templeton as laid-back, relaxed and happy about acting in his little charade. Besides, knowing his type—arrogant and rich—Ross Templeton would probably appear in the lobby of his hotel outfitted in full tycoon regalia. No way was she going to bop in wearing a pair of faded jeans.

She got out her nicest darkest suit and laid it out on the chair to put on. Then she folded one so similar it could have been its twin into a garment bag. She made quick work of stuffing her small weekend suitcase with underclothes, extra shoes and panty hose.

She glanced up at the clock. Only fifteen minutes to dress and finish packing! She'd wasted far too much time this afternoon stewing about Ross Templeton.

The man was truly heart-stoppingly handsome. Just looking into those baby blues of his made her toes curl. Keeping up her nun routine with this man was going to be difficult.

Then again, with a man that rich and good-looking, keeping up her nun routine was essential.

Initially she'd had every intention of telling him the truth about her nun status. That was before she almost ran a red light on the way home—because, she realized with dismay, she'd been daydreaming about a disarming pair of blue eyes. Being a nun would provide just the protection she needed from whatever residual weakness she had for hunks in suits. Wes had taught her an invaluable lesson—not to trust a man handsome enough to make your head spin. She didn't need Ross to provide her with a diploma.

Not that he seemed the least bit interested in her—aside from what function she could serve in his baby charade. He was too caught up in his own problems to take notice of anyone else. If he wasn't so self-absorbed, he might have taken a good look at her and realized she couldn't possibly be a nun, even though she had lived like one, figuratively, for a year. It seemed like forever since she'd even thought of a man in a romantic light.

Although, now that she considered the matter, if she was going to think of a man that way, Ross *was* an awfully delectable specimen. She remembered his rusty dark hair and wondered what it would be like to comb her fingers through it....

The doorbell rang and she hopped up, startled out of her thoughts—which were pretty startling to begin with.

Sister Joan, with Felicity beside her in her stroller, stood alert on her front stoop when Alison opened the door. The nun's eyes widened in dismay as she gave

Alison a once-over. "Oh, my. Still in your bathrobe! Did I come too early?"

"No, no," Alison stammered, embarrassed. "I'm really almost ready."

Sister Joan bustled past her. "I'll just help myself to a cup of coffee, then. Or better still, a cola. You do keep cola in the fridge, don't you?"

Grunting an assent, Alison followed the nun, who seemed instinctively to know the way to the kitchen. The small woman hesitated only long enough to call over her shoulder, "Don't forget Felicity!"

Alison turned back to the baby, still sitting in her stroller by the door, looking none too pleased at being left behind. Alison feared this slight would get their weekend together off to a bad start and half expected the kid to break out into a wail of indignation.

But she didn't.

Alison looked warily from Felicity to the kitchen, where she could hear Sister Joan banging about. "I don't know which of you to distrust more," she grumbled under her breath.

Felicity gurgled testily in response.

"What was that, dear?" Sister Joan called.

Alison got behind the stroller and pushed Felicity to the kitchen. "I was just telling Felicity here that I'd better hurry up and get dressed."

"Oh, yes, go right ahead," Sister Joan told her, her Reeboks making soft squeaky sounds on the linoleum as she went to inspect the contents of Alison's cabinets. "I can manage in here just fine. Oh, Cheerios!" She clapped her hands together with glee, then explained, "We never get that kind of cereal at the convent. But I guess you know that."

Alison didn't need to be reminded of the lumpy oatmeal she'd downed for five mornings straight.

"Be my guest," she said unnecessarily. From the sound of silver clanging against pottery, she guessed Sister Joan had already found the bowls and spoons.

Alison padded back to her room and made quick work of dressing.

Moments later Sister Joan, standing in the doorway, gaped at her with such shock that Alison feared the cereal bowl would slip right out of her hands. "You're not wearing *that,* are you?"

She glanced down at her dark suit, hose and pumps and shrugged. "It's what I always wear."

"That's just what's wrong," Sister Joan said, making a beeline for Alison's garment bag. When she unzipped it, she nearly howled at the similar suit Alison had packed. "Merciful heavens! Not another one! Do you sleep in them, too?"

Alison rolled her eyes. "If you look closely, you'll see I packed a nightgown."

Immediately a high-necked thick cotton garment was produced from her suitcase. "*This* is a nightgown?" Sister Joan bellowed in disgust.

"In case you've forgotten, I'm supposed to be a nun."

The distasteful look on Sister Joan's face didn't go away. She held the gown at arm's length. "It's things like this that give nuns a bad reputation."

The stiff flannel *did* appear more unbreachable than a medieval fortress. Becoming self-conscious, Alison rescued her nightie from the disapproving nun. "I bought it—and packed it—because it was comfortable."

Before she could make a thorough defense of her

nightwear, Sister Joan discovered Alison's dresser and startled rifling through its drawers, picking out items willy-nilly and tossing them toward the bed. Her small form disappeared behind a flying cloud of jeans, T-shirts and silky lingerie. "You'll thank me for this!" she hollered over Alison's cries of protest. The neat bedroom was suddenly a whirlwind jumble of clothes—only a few of which had actually landed on the bed. Garments hung from lamps and a chair and littered the floor; the room looked as if a retail blizzard had hit. Sister Joan picked up clothes randomly and began making a shambles of Alison's packing job.

"Please," Alison begged, feeling the last vestiges of calm and control being ripped out from under her. "I packed *very* carefully."

"Ha!" the older woman scoffed.

"Wait!" Alison cried, pulling out a slinky red teddy Sister Joan had thrown in. She felt embarrassed just looking at the thing, which was a product of too many lonely Friday nights spent with a bottle of wine and the Victoria's Secret catalog. She'd never gathered up the courage to wear it as far as her living room.

"That is hardly appropriate, and I'm sure I won't need—"

Sister Joan cut her off with a sharp reproach, punctuated with two balled fists on her hips. "Have you forgotten Felicity again?"

Confused, Alison blinked. "Felicity?"

"You parked her in the kitchen, dear," the nun lectured. "You really shouldn't leave her unattended for long."

The nun was already barking out more orders as Alison ran to retrieve the baby.

"You'd better hurry if you're going to be on time

to meet Mr. Templeton! He was most adamant about getting off on time. Poor man, he's in such a hurry to get back to his dear father.''

As Alison ran into the kitchen to find Felicity kicking her chubby legs impatiently in her stroller, she heard Sister Joan call out, ''Oh, my, what a mess! You'll need to tidy up before you go!''

Sister Joan made it sound as if she had no idea *who* had created such a mess. Alison turned to express her displeasure when suddenly a piercing shriek was sent up from the stroller's pudgy-cheeked occupant. Alison's gaze was now riveted on Felicity, whose face had turned a perfect Stop-sign red. She immediately leaned down to pick up the infant, but Felicity's back stiffened in response, her little fists swiping at the air in front of her in fury.

''What's the matter, baby?'' Alison asked, attempting a soothing tone, although she was forced to coo at high volume to be heard over Felicity's cries.

''Oh, dear...'' Sister Joan, appearing in the doorway, muttered.

Alison turned, a little frightened by the sister's ominous tone. ''What?''

The nun quickly tried to feign nonchalance. ''Oh, I'm sure it's nothing.''

''What?'' Alison insisted.

''It's just...'' Sister Joan sighed. ''Well, the last time Felicity looked like this, it took three days to calm her down.''

ROSS TAPPED HIS FOOT impatiently and glanced at his watch for the zillionth time. Where the heck was that nun with his baby? Sister Alison hadn't struck him as the type to be late.

Since taking leave of her, he'd convinced himself he picked exactly the right woman to accompany him—as long as he kept his eyes off her legs. And ignored the sway of her hips. And didn't stare too long into those big brown eyes of hers.

She'd seemed a no-nonsense nun, which was fine with him. He didn't need any fussy female goings-on muddying the waters. It was hard enough just dealing with his father's illness without also having some flaky lady on his hands. Ross just wanted to narrow his focus to that baby and making his father happy.

So where was Sister Alison?

As the persistent question echoed, so did the sound of a high-pitched baby's wail. It grew louder, and Ross pivoted to see Sister Alison striding toward him full tilt, the red-faced baby swaddled in her arms. The hotel doorman—weighed down with a small suitcase and garment bag, the car seat and a huge pink shoulder bag of baby paraphernalia—trailed after her.

The nun was dressed in a stiff navy business suit and matching pumps, which struck Ross as oddly businesslike. But then again, before this afternoon he'd never heard of nuns running modeling agencies. He supposed he had a lot to learn about the modern world of religious orders. He himself was outfitted in weekend attire—jeans, boots and a long-sleeved polo shirt—a fact that seemed not to escape the uncomfortable-looking Sister Alison as she approached him.

His eyes looked into hers. Big mistake. Even as she gazed at him in a slightly hostile fashion, he felt a zip of attraction to her. Good grief! He needed to get a grip.

Tend to your business. And the most important business he had right now was his baby. His gaze fixed on the scarlet pinched-up face squinting out from a downy blanket decorated with lavender bunnies. *That* was the adorable little girl he had found this afternoon?

"What did you do to her?"

The nun's harried expression became a mask of defensiveness. "*I* haven't done anything!" she insisted. "*You* were the one who let yourself be swindled into taking this baby on your twisted mission of mercy."

He should have known they would be at each other's throats seconds after meeting again. "We have a long trip ahead of us, Sister. It would help if you didn't start by telling me my business. Today this little girl was the picture of sweetness. What's the matter with her?"

Alison's lips screwed up tersely. "I believe she's crying."

Ross's jaw clenched. "I can see that. Did you try to find out why?"

"I've asked her, but she refuses to tell me."

A drop-dead gorgeous, smart-aleck nun. Terrific. This was going to be a great weekend.

"Did you change her diaper? That sometimes—"

"Yes, I did." Alison shifted the baby to her opposite shoulder, patting her lightly on the back. "Frankly I'm beginning to believe there's only one explanation for all these tears."

Ross was slightly surprised she could sound so calm if she'd been listening to this wailing for any length of time. "And that is?"

"This baby's in a very bad mood."

He huffed out an impatient breath. "That's impossible. A little thing like her? I thought…I mean, babies don't…"

A dark eyebrow rose up with interest as his words sputtered and died. "Yes, Dr. Spock?"

"Oh, hell," he muttered, reaching over. "Give her to me." He took the baby in his arms and mumbled an uncomfortable, "Hey there, little girl!"

Cradled in his large hands and probably surprised by her sudden change in elevation, Felicity sucked in a fitful breath and gazed up at her new person. At least she stopped crying.

"See there?" Ross asked uneasily. "You just have to talk to her a little bit."

Sister Alison crossed her arms. "Is that right?"

"Sure," he said, his confidence building as the startling hue of red in the little face looking up at him began to fade to a healthier pink. He bounced the baby gently, as if she were a piece of heirloom crystal. "Little Felicity just needed some TLC."

After a tiny hiccup, Felicity opened her mouth wide and a cry erupted from her like hot lava from Mount Vesuvius. Her face was soon the color of hot lava, too.

Sister Alison looked at Ross sagely. "As you were saying...?"

"Take her, won't you?" he said, handing her over.

Arms crossed over her chest, a cool grin playing across her lips, Alison shook her head. "Oh, I think you're doing just about as well as I could. And since you're so gung ho about playing daddy, it's probably good practice for you."

For the first time he looked self-consciously around and saw to his chagrin that every soul in the hotel's usually serene lobby was staring at them. "Come on," he urged, scowling as he awkwardly cradled the baby in one hand and bent down to pick up his briefcase.

He nodded to the porter, then toward the lobby's front doors. "My car's out this way." He started walking, then stopped abruptly, almost causing his entourage to collide with him.

He shifted Felicity and his briefcase and reached into his breast pocket. "I had a list of things to check off, so we wouldn't have to stop..."

Sister Alison rolled her eyes. "You can put away the list, Mr. Templeton. That Business 101 stuff might work with hotels, but if there's one thing I've learned from working with kids, it's that you *always* have to stop."

He frowned but, ceding her point, reluctantly turned and began walking again. Sister Alison and the porter followed suit. With Felicity trumpeting their progress, he led the way out to where an attendant stood by a forest green Jaguar.

The nun stopped in front of it. "Nice car."

"It's just a rental," Ross explained, taking the keys from the attendant as he awkwardly dug into his pocket for a tip.

"I take it you don't get your rentals from Rent-a-Wreck."

He supposed that was meant to be a caustic comment on his lavish lifestyle. "I make no apologies for having a weakness for fast cars."

She smiled broadly over the sports car's high-gloss roof, and even aware of how annoyed he was by her and the baby and everything, he couldn't help thinking how beautiful she was. How un-nunlike. "Now that you're a family man, don't you think you ought to slow down?"

He grinned back. "When and if I do slow down, I intend to do it in style."

He was gratified that Sister Alison at least leaned into the back seat from the passenger side and helped him put in the child seat and then strap Felicity into it. Afterward he collapsed exhaustedly into his own seat and turned to her. Felicity was still crying. His head was beginning to feel numb from the persistent noise.

"I suppose it would be too much to ask for her to be a good traveler."

Sister Alison nodded. "Much too much."

Felicity bellowed her agreement.

Once they were encased inside the car, which was upholstered in a rich brown leather, the sound of the baby's wails became even more distracting. Ross took a deep breath. Next to him he sensed Sister Alison letting out a sigh.

"I tried to warn you," she said, leaning over her seat into the back in an attempt to get the baby to accept a pacifier.

As Ross suspected, their little darling was binky-proof.

"All I remember is your telling me how unethical my plan was." He turned on the engine. Felicity brayed in response to the new sound. "You never said anything about the damage it might cause my ear-drums. Or my nerves."

"If you'd given me time to explain, I would have gotten down to the nuts and bolts behind my disagree-ment. But you wouldn't listen."

He couldn't believe he was sniping with a nun.

"Under the circumstances, maybe you ought to practice just calling me Alison."

"All right, Alison." Somehow, calling her that seemed almost blasphemous, and way too intimate. He glanced sideways and caught the corners of her mouth turning up in a smile. Ruefully he smiled back. "You'd better call me Ross."

"Okay." She shrugged. "At least we know we bicker very believably."

"Right," Ross agreed. "In fact, we sound more like an old married couple than sweethearts."

"Truce," she said, smiling at him.

He looked so long at her red-tinted lips stretching over a set of perfect white teeth that he almost veered the Jaguar into a ditch.

Good heavens, what was the matter with him?

He harrumphed in consternation as he took the on-ramp to the freeway and headed toward the open, yet very crowded Dallas road. Maybe once they were on the interstate, the car wouldn't be jarred so much and Felicity would go to sleep. As he shifted into fifth gear, his hand brushed Alison's thigh. Both of them jumped about three feet, and two bright red stains appeared in Alison's cheeks.

Marvelous! He would have liked to believe that they were simply edgy from the crying baby, but the familiar tightening in his gut as he watched Alison reach down and pull her wool skirt over her long shapely legs gave lie to that hope. Alison the nun, despite her best efforts, was sexy.

He trained his gaze back on the road. Damn. There must be something wrong with him. He hadn't dated any woman steadily since Cara. Now he wondered if that hadn't been a mistake. When a man started lusting after nuns, it was time he got out more.

He felt his gaze slipping back over to Alison. If he didn't watch out, he would scare her away and end up childless by the time they reached the city limits.

Focus, Ross, he coached himself. He'd made a lot of money for his family by knowing how to keep ferociously on task. He'd heard the word headstrong linked to his name. His own father had often accused him of being too rigid, too intent on getting what he wanted. But this time what he wanted wasn't just for himself. He wanted this baby for his father.

"Where are you going?"

Ross turned to see Alison, her hands tensed on the armrests, looking at the road ahead in alarm. "What?"

"This isn't the way to the airport," she pointed out.

"I know that."

"Then where are we headed?" she demanded.

"West Texas."

She turned to him, her eyes wide and very very displeased. She didn't loosen her grip on the armrests, either. Ross noticed that she wore bright red nail polish. He found it strangely intriguing...and curious.

"We're *driving* all the way to your father's ranch?"

"That's right."

"You said we were going to fly!"

"There was a problem with the jet's engine, so there's been a change in plan. A nuisance of course, but... Didn't Sister Joan tell you?"

"No." She looked out her window and muttered, "Naturally."

"When you weren't in your office this afternoon, I called St. Felicity's and informed her of the switch."

"That Sister Joan!" She shook her head, beginning to appear a little frantic. "Why don't we try to get a commercial flight? Wouldn't that save time?"

"Not really. The ranch is remote, and flights out to the nearest little airfield don't leave very often—and not at all when the weather's bad."

Alison looked up and checked out the dark clouds hanging overhead. There was also a blustery wind that could have caused some problems. "But this doesn't make sense. Driving…"

"Is faster," he finished for her.

She swung around in a huff. "I demand that you stop this car," she said over the baby's howls.

"Absolutely not."

"B-but I don't even know the slightest thing about you—even if you have a valid license."

Laughing, he reached around and dug into his hip pocket for his wallet. "Here are my credentials." He tossed his driver's license over to her.

She gave the card a good going-over, almost as if she hoped to find something wrong with it. "I guess that's you, all right," she said glumly after a few moments. Then her eyebrows raised with interest. "You're really thirty-five?"

He nodded. "Something wrong with that?"

"You strike me as a much younger man."

"Thirty-five isn't exactly over the hill."

"No, but…"

"But what?"

"Well, so far all I know about you is that you have a spoiled boy's headstrong ideas about getting what he wants and an interest in cars that are expensive enough to feed, house and clothe a family of five for a year. In my book, that shows a certain lack of maturity."

He managed to keep the Jaguar's course straight in spite of the annoyance her barbs caused him. "I prefer to think of myself as young at heart, Sister."

His unruffled feathers irked her, and she tossed his license back over to him. "Alison, remember?"

"Right. And we're supposed to be trying to get along, remember?"

She bristled at his reprimand, which was punctuated by a fresh set of wails from the back seat. That kid had better lung power than Pavarotti.

"Excuse me if I'm a little rattled to discover I'm going to be cooped up in a car all evening," she said. "I wish I could convince you to turn this car around and forget all about this foolhardy idea."

"Don't count on it," Ross told her. "Sorry if my plan doesn't measure up to your high ethical standards, Alison, but you *did* agree to take my money."

As if sensing defeat, she sank low in her seat. "I only did it for the sake of the convent."

For a moment the car was again consumed by the fretful crying coming from the back. "Poor baby," Alison said, turning. "What are we going to do with you for a whole six hours?"

Now that he and Alison were at a standoff, Ross was feeling almost as fitful as the kid. "How about some music?" he suggested, wishing to listen to anything but the sound of a baby's cries and Sister Alison's intermittent lectures. "What do you like to listen to?"

Alison turned forward again enthusiastically. The dancing glint in her eyes made it obvious that she also viewed music as a welcome diversion. "Oh, you know, the usual. Oldies, mostly. The Stones, Van Morrison, Dylan..."

Ross's mouth dropped open in surprise. "Dylan?"

She glanced at him, puzzled. "Yeah, so?"

"I mean, aren't those musicians rather...unorthodox?"

Alison paled. "Oh, I see. Well..." She cleared her

throat. "Actually, when I said oldies, I was really thinking about *old* oldies—you know, like classical music. Bach, Beethoven and all those guys. Gosh, I love that stuff."

Ross laughed. "Right," he said, not believing a word of it. "I think I just discovered Sister Alison's secret passion."

He detected a faint blush in her cheeks. "Whatever you want to listen to is fine with me. Of course, I really *would* prefer a classical station..." Her voice trailed off as he fiddled with the knob.

In the end he couldn't get good reception on the classical station, but the oldies station came in great. Soon the Jaguar was zooming down the interstate to the sound of the Rolling Stones' "Satisfaction."

"Is this okay?" he asked.

She shrugged. "Fine."

Despite Alison's attempt to appear uninterested, Ross detected some subtle foot tapping from the passenger side of the car. She leaned back in her seat, looking as relaxed as a person could with a baby crying in her ears.

Ross wondered if he wasn't beginning to understand Alison a little better. She might be a nun—but she was a nun with contradictions.

Wondering whether this was good or bad—and whether he should care one way or the other how Sister Alison felt about her vocation—Ross drove on. Finally, at the beginning of a slow Barbra Streisand ballad, he felt the urge to break the silence between them. "Say, Alison..."

No response. He looked over and discovered that Alison's head had dropped to the side. She was snoozing as deeply as he'd ever witnessed someone snoozing in a car. What was more, he realized as he basked in the precious silence in the car, a miracle had occurred.

The baby was asleep, too!

He hadn't noticed exactly when it had happened—probably sometime between "Satisfaction" and "I Heard It through the Grapevine." Now the only sound coming from baby Felicity was a contented gurgle. Beside him, Alison emitted a soft snore. Ross smiled. Both nun and child seemed to harbor a secret love of golden oldies.

He sank down in his seat, allowing himself to relax a little for the first time since he'd heard the news about his father.

Dad. This whole expedition was for the old man, yet except for checking in regularly with the hospital, it seemed he had been thinking very little about his father's condition. Maybe because the thought of living in a world without Henry Templeton was just too painful for him to contemplate right now. Instead, he was preoccupied with plans of how he was going to pass off this baby as his, as well as unsettling thoughts about the woman at his side.

What had he been about to ask her? Ross racked his brains as he became mesmerized by the landscape whizzing past and the dulcet tones of Barbra singing "Evergreen." Then it came to him, the question as random and nonsensical as the words to the song.

How many nuns at St. Felicity's wore flame red nail polish?

Chapter Three

''Alison? Alison, wake up. We're here.''

Still half-asleep, Alison smiled. Like a flower to morning sunlight, her body seemed to stretch instinctively toward the deep voice saying her name. She slowly let her eyes flutter open—then felt her smile abruptly disappear.

It was dark outside, but through the interior light of the car, two faces peered at her. First there was Ross, his gaze curious and a little insistent. How long had she been asleep—and how long had he been watching her? Then she noticed he was holding Felicity on his lap. The baby was staring at her impatiently. Alison tensed, preparing for a wail to disrupt the almost eerie silence around her.

''How long has she been that way?'' she asked tentatively, afraid any sudden movement or sound might upset the blessed peace.

Ross smiled. ''Since approximately the same time you fell asleep three and a half hours ago.''

''Three and a half hours!'' She shot up in her seat, disoriented. She remembered Ross saying, ''We're here,'' but he'd explained earlier that his father's ranch was a six-hour drive from Dallas. So where was "here"?

Outside, a small one-story brick building boasted a sign that read, "Darla's Dinner Bell—Good Food." Other than that, they appeared to be in the middle of nowhere with nothing but open pasture around them. The empty highway stretched its gray length in both directions as far as the eye could see. There was one other vehicle in the parking lot, a pickup truck that, unless she missed her guess, probably belonged to Darla.

"I could stand a bite to eat," Ross said, "and I bet we could all use some time outside this car."

Felicity batted an adorable little fist in the air in full agreement.

As if on cue, Alison's stomach rumbled hungrily. But she wasn't taking a step outside the car until she discovered what Ross had been up to.

"Wait a second," she said, poking a finger toward Felicity. "I want to know what kind of voodoo you've performed on that baby."

He smiled, looking equal parts handsome and silly with the sweet-faced cherub in his arms and the big pink baby bag slung over his shoulder. "No supernatural powers were necessary. It turns out that Felicity, you and I have something in common."

"What's that?"

"A love of golden oldies."

Alison tilted her head skeptically.

"It's true," Ross went on. "You both conked out to Marvin Gaye."

She still wasn't convinced. During the diaper-commercial shoot, they had tried everything to quiet the child, including every food imaginable, nursery rhymes, toys, prayers…

But they hadn't tried Marvin Gaye. Or any other oldies songs.

She looked at Felicity and, tentatively, hummed a few bars of Van Morrison's "Brown-Eyed Girl."

Felicity's wet pudgy lips flopped open for a moment as she listened to the song. Then, to Alison's surprise, she burst into peals of giggles.

Alison drew back in wonder. "It works!" Who'd have thought?

Ross looked more smug than if he'd just solved the riddle of the Sphinx or the mystery of Dennis Rodman's hair. "Told you."

To give the devil his due, the man had made a key discovery. Between that and the most solid sleep she'd had for five straight days, Alison felt decidedly better. "Dinner it is," she assented, unfolding herself from the low front seat.

Ross carried Felicity and her diaper bag into the restaurant, which gave a whole new meaning to the term greasy spoon. The place, though clean, was sparsely decorated in that stunning avocado shade that was all the rage back in 1974. The air was redolent with the aroma from meat loaf of yore.

At least, Alison hoped it was yore.

She slid into a vinyl booth. "Are you sure you're ready to tackle feeding?" she asked as Ross placed the car seat in the booth next to him and picked Felicity up. He bounced her and hummed a Credence Clearwater Revival tune.

"Sure. After my success with finding the right music for a six-month-old, my confidence is growing by leaps and bounds."

"This might be a little more involved than turning a radio knob."

He sent her a knowing smirk as he fished out one of the bottles Sister Joan had packed. "You just relax and enjoy your meal, Alison. Women don't have a monopoly on feeding kids, you know."

"Okay, but don't say I didn't warn you."

She sighed and glanced at the menu that had been stuck behind the salt-and-pepper-shaker holder. The list was limited to typical roadside fare, but since she hadn't had a bite to eat since her lumpy oatmeal at St. Felicity's that morning, she was hardly in a mood to be picky.

Eventually a woman clad in jeans, sneakers, an orange cap and matching apron sauntered out. Underneath that cap, her hair was blond right out of a bottle. She looked out the window next to them and whistled. "Whooo—ee! That's one fancy car, mister. What are you—an oil tycoon?"

"No, just a hotel tycoon," Alison quipped.

"No kiddin'?" the waitress asked, turning to Ross. "My brother Earl owns a hotel. Earl's Motel, it's called. Just down the road. Me and him's the only two businesses in town."

Alison and Ross's eyes met in confusion. "Where's the town?" he asked.

Darla sent him a you've-got-to-be-joking glance. "Ya'll must be coming from the east, otherwise you woulda seen the sign out by the hotel. This here's Woodard, on account of I'm Darla Woodard and my family started the town. But it's dwindled some since the economy crashed."

"You mean in the late eighties?" Ross asked.

"Nope, I mean back in the late twenties," Darla

said, emitting a cackle of delight that let them know they weren't the first ones she'd had this particular exchange with. "Ya'll see anything to tempt your tastebuds?"

"I'll have a cheeseburger," Alison said without hesitation.

"Me, too," Ross chimed in.

"And what about for your friend here?" Darla leaned down and chucked Felicity under her chubby chin. "Say, aren't you the cutest little thing? You oughta be in show business!"

"She's just having formula," Alison said, not even wanting to think about babies and their professional careers for at least two days. "Although she might need some extra napkins."

Darla shook her head. "I guess any kid with two such good-lookin' parents would have to turn out decent, right?"

For a moment Alison sat with her mouth agape, not sure if she'd heard right. The heat that crept into her cheeks within moments confirmed that she had. "Oh, no. I mean, we're not—"

"Two cheeseburgers comin' right up," Darla said, turning and sauntering back toward the kitchen.

Alison's mouth snapped closed and she turned to Ross to gauge his reaction. He laughed. "It's an honest mistake, you know. We're a couple with a baby."

"I know, but we're not—"

He didn't wait for her to state the obvious. "If anything, it makes me feel better that she made that mistake. Now if only my father makes the same one, everything will be fine."

"Your father won't have to come to any conclusions, since you plan to lie to him flat out,'' Alison said tartly.

''I take it after your soothing nap you still don't approve of my plan?''

''Not in the least.'' Alison lifted her head. ''In fact, the closer we get, the guiltier I feel. I have half a mind to tell your father the truth!''

His eyes narrowed on her. ''You do that and St. Felicity's won't see a dime of my money. I'll put a stop payment on my check. We have a bargain. If you don't intend to stick to it, you should say so now.''

She sighed unhappily. Blackmail was a bummer. ''Of course I'll stick to it. But there's no reason I have to pretend to think you're Mr. Wonderful, is there?''

''Pretend?'' He screwed his face up quizzically. ''No, I would think that would come naturally.''

''Very funny.'' Alison shook her head. What an egomaniac! He was probably used to women falling at his feet.

She took a calming sip of water before looking up at Ross again. He was staring at her strangely. ''What?'' she asked, wondering whether her lipstick had smudged.

''Nothing,'' he answered quickly.

She glared at him insistently. ''No, you were looking at me funny. What was it?''

''Okay,'' he admitted, ''if you must know, I was thinking how pretty you are.''

''What?'' she practically shrieked.

He lifted his forefinger to his lip and made a shushing sound. ''You'll disturb Felicity.''

Since Felicity was blissfully sucking on her bottle, Alison made the concession of lowering her voice.

"What in heaven's name put a thought like that into your head?"

"Are you telling me you don't like to be complimented?"

Alison blinked. Not like it? A part of her was lapping it up. The part she'd been trying to squelch for almost a year.

I'm a nun, she reminded herself.

She'd rather eat toads than let Ross Templeton know how well his flattery worked. She looked into his eyes and saw that same arrogance she'd been too naive to notice in Wes—the certainty that he was far too sexy for his own good. Too sexy for *her* own good.

Darla came back and slung their plates in front of them. "Can I get ya'll anything else?"

"I'll have a beer," Alison said. She definitely needed cooling down.

"Sure thing, hon," Darla said, turning away.

Ross stared at Alison the entire time it took Darla to retrieve and deliver the beverage. He watched Alison intently as she took her first long swig.

"Wow, that's good," she said. She was beginning to feel awkward under his steady gaze. "Anything wrong?"

"A beer?" he asked.

Mindful of Darla's presence on the other side of the swinging door that led to the kitchen, she whispered, "I'm a nun, not a saint."

She was beginning to be a pretty good liar, too. A few more days and even *she* might be convinced she was a nun.

"I can see that," he said, looking sexier than ought

to be allowed while eating a greasy cheeseburger with one hand and feeding a baby with the other.

She shifted uncomfortably in the vinyl booth. ''What's that supposed to mean?''

He shrugged. ''Just that you seem to be one of the most unconventional nuns I've ever run across.''

''Have you run across many?'' she asked, holding her breath.

He laughed. ''Exactly none, actually. I come from a long line of Methodists. All I know about convents is what I've seen in the movies. You know—*The Sound of Music,* and that thing with Audrey Hepburn.''

Alison bridled at the last movie reference, the same one that had suckered her in. ''You can't believe movies,'' she said, speaking from bitter experience. ''Nuns today have to live in the real world.'' *Or a twisted version thereof,* she amended silently, remembering her week at St. Felicity's.

He nodded toward her hand. ''Including certain vanities like nail polish?''

She looked down at her hands and struggled to find a reason a nun would be wearing such an outlandish color. She failed.

He studied her for a long moment, then announced, ''I know your secret, Alison.''

He knows!

When had he guessed? Her heart beat like a gerbil's during the interminable moments he stared at her with a lopsided grin on his face. How was she going to spend a weekend with this man if she couldn't hide behind her nun disguise?

And why, oh why, hadn't she thought to remove her nail polish?

She swallowed, then croaked, "S-secret?"

"You're a misfit."

Alison blinked.

A misfit? Was that all?

She breathed a sigh of relief and started dabbing her greasy french fries with a paper napkin.

"I could tell from the way Sister Joan spoke about you. That head nun at St. Felicity's—what's her name?"

"Sister Catherine," Alison supplied, popping a fry into her mouth. It was still greasier than an oil slick. It was great.

"I got the feeling your superiors think the life for you there is too...confining."

"Everyone has to deal with life's limitations. And I have a lot more freedom than some nuns."

Ross looked frustrated. "But don't you want more? I would go crazy being told what I could and couldn't do."

Alison remembered her week at the convent, during which she'd been at the edge of going completely bonkers. She smiled inwardly at the calm she was able to muster now and said in cool measured tones, "One learns to prize obedience above all."

She could hear his foot tapping impatiently. "I could understand that coming from Sister Joan."

She raised a brow. "Why not me?"

"Because you're so young, so...so normal. You like music and makeup and cheeseburgers."

"So do a lot of nuns."

"But I can't be completely wrong." He fidgeted, then said, "I mean, the way you look at me sometimes..."

Alison's face became a four-alarm blaze and she quickly popped three more fries into her mouth.

"Don't you miss..." He looked at her, then looked away.

Alison swallowed. "Go ahead," she urged, all the while hoping to goodness he would drop the subject.

Those blue eyes bore into hers. "Don't you miss...sex?"

For a moment her heart palpitated so, she thought she might faint. *I'm a nun, I'm a nun...*

And, more important, she'd sworn off men like Ross.

Yet at some level she was bowled over that Ross Templeton was interested in her sex life, or complete lack of one. Much the same way she had been flattered when Wes had twinkled his baby blues at her the first time. This devilish curiosity for the opposite sex was precisely the reason she could never really be a nun—but desperately needed to pretend to be.

Slowly, as the silence stretched between them, Ross began to look as if he wanted to crawl under a rock. He glanced down solemnly at Felicity and said, "I'm sorry. I didn't intend to sound as if... I mean, I know you must be a..."

She almost laughed at his discomfort. "A what?" she asked, blinking innocently.

"Well..." His face turned beet red. And he was *still* handsome! "A *virgin.*"

At least she still had the upper hand, Alison thought, not without glee. She could afford to be generous. "I wasn't raised in a convent, you know."

This time he blinked—in astonishment. "You mean you're not a..."

She took a deep breath, thought briefly of Wes and

answered, "To tell you the truth, my experience with serious romance wasn't all that gratifying."

His eyebrows rose in curiosity. "Really?"

God, she loved a man who liked to talk. Some men were so closemouthed they didn't even know important details about their best friends or even their lovers. Wes was like that. And he was even more tight-lipped about himself. Which might explain why she had been so completely stunned when he left her standing at the altar with a wilting bouquet in her hand.

But perhaps Ross felt he could speak more freely because "Sister Alison" was completely out of bounds.

"I was almost married once," she said. "But I wasn't in love—not really. And the man turned out to be a rat. So, in the end, it was all for the best. But it didn't exactly prime me to go looking for more love."

"Except the kind you could find through the church," Ross finished for her.

"Well, yes." Now that it was out, her explanation for joining the convent seemed rather pat. If every woman who was the victim of a hard-luck romance became a nun, the earth's population would dwindle to zero in nothing flat. "Of course, I'd felt a calling to my vocation for a long time before that. Wes was just the—"

"Straw that broke the camel's back?"

She nodded. Did the man ever let a person finish a sentence?

Ross ate the final bite of his burger and shifted Felicity in his lap. His forehead was crinkled in thought. "Okay," he conceded, "but what if you find someone else?"

She shook her head, knowing exactly where this

was leading—somewhere she definitely didn't want to go. "I'm not looking."

His blue eyes glinted in challenge. "What if you just happened to be thrown together with someone for a while?"

She swallowed. *I'm a nun. Oh, Lord, I'm a nun...* "The point is, I look at people differently now."

"But you're still human. If you did pass up an opportunity to have a relationship with this hypothetical person, wouldn't you always wonder what might have been?"

"I suppose so," she said, exasperated. "As you say, I'm human. But the fact is, I'm not looking for romantic love. So this whole conversation is pointless."

She finished her sentence by stuffing enough fries in her mouth to make her cheeks bulge like a chipmunk's. She hated the edge in her voice, but she didn't really think she could stand talking about matters of love with a person who was absolutely the last man in the world she should fall in love with.

Luckily Darla came back to the table to ask them if they wanted dessert, putting an end to the uncomfortable conversation.

"Just the check," Ross said.

Darla plunked the tab on the table, and Ross, balancing an unhappy-looking Felicity on his knee, fished through his wallet.

Alison looked warily at Felicity, who, supported by only one of Ross's tanned manicured hands, wobbled precariously. "I don't think you should hold her like that."

Ross plunked enough money to cover dinner and a tip on the table. He seemed tense. "I'm not going to let her drop, if that's what you mean."

"I just—"

Before she could issue her warning, however, it was too late. In the blink of an eye, Felicity's dinner was all over Ross's shirt.

"Good grief!" Ross yelled, jumping back. To his credit, he *didn't* drop her. Felicity erupted again, this time in wails. He glared at Alison, as if all this was *her* fault. "What do I do now?"

Alison bit back a smile. "Change your shirt, for starters."

His lips pursed in displeasure. "Very funny."

He really looked peeved. Then again, recalling her own damaged wardrobe, she knew a little about how he felt. "I'll take her," Alison offered.

He handed the baby over gingerly, then stood up. "I'll have to get a shirt out of the car," he grumbled.

"Felicity and I will wait for you here."

His head bobbed curtly and she watched him stomp to the door, amazed that he wasn't recovering his equilibrium faster. After all, what was a shirt to a man with as much money as Ross had?

She frowned in thought. Or maybe his bad temper had nothing to do with Felicity. She remembered that he had seemed peevish ever since she ended their conversation about her lack of interest in the opposite sex.

Could it be that Ross was disappointed?

Why? Because a nun wouldn't let him seduce her?

At least the man could never be accused of underestimating his charm.

WHY EVERYONE INSISTED that babies needed two-parent families soon became obvious to Ross. It was a law that babies had to ride in car seats. And strapping a wiggling, fussy little body into one of the blasted things was pretty much a two-person job. By the time he finally had Felicity battened down, beads of perspiration had broken out on his brow, the baby was cranky again, and Alison, who had decided to visit the ladies' room after Ross had changed his shirt, was still nowhere in sight.

What was she doing in there—writing the great American novel on toilet paper?

He leaned against the Jag, took a deep gulp of warm night air and tried to master his impatience, which had nothing to do with Felicity's gastric indiscretion and everything to do with Alison. He knew full well why she was loath to return to the cramped confines of the car. He'd scared her away with all his talk of romance and what-ifs.

No wonder she'd run from him like he was the living incarnation of the Ebola virus. In retrospect, he wanted to give himself a swift kick in the pants.

For years he'd avoided entanglements, which, in truth, hadn't even been all that difficult. After Cara he hadn't exactly been pining for another serious relationship. Work was more rewarding, and a few careful casual flings were a lot more fun.

So why, when he finally did find himself fixated on a certain woman, did it have to be a nun? Was he a masochist?

He certainly felt like one. He also felt like a damn fool for questioning her like he had at dinner. The poor woman must think he was a nut. He was beginning to think so, too. What was most frustrating, though, was that it almost seemed to him as if Sister Alison *was* interested in him, despite her protests to the contrary. Which might prove nothing aside from the fact that his sexual radar was rusty from disuse.

But could there be any mistaking that tug of attraction between a man and a woman? That look of curiosity in the eyes? That floppy feeling in the stomach when you realized the person you were eyeing had their feelers out, too?

Heaven help him, he'd been sensing weird vibes coming off Alison all day. What was worse, he found himself responding to these probably nonexistent signals, even though every fiber in his being screamed that he was being a complete nincompoop. When Alison had described the failed romance that led her to take a vow of chastity, he'd felt a strong desire to hunt down the man who'd hurt her and wring his sorry neck.

At that moment Alison appeared. He couldn't see her very well, but when her long-legged stroll had eaten up most of the distance to the car, he noted that she had removed her suit jacket and was now sporting only the silky sleeveless shell she'd been wearing underneath. Combined with her above-the-knee-length skirt, the outfit was unnervingly slinky.

His expression turned grim. "Are you sure you're a nun?"

Her eyes popped open in surprise, and she stared at him, shocked. "What?" she asked primly.

"Never mind," he muttered, giving himself a mental kick. "I just don't know why the hell I couldn't have found an order of nuns who still wore long robes and wimples."

She gawked at him for another moment, then swiveled toward the back seat. "I'm sorry, Ross. I didn't mean for you to do all the work."

He forced himself to turn away from the pale slender curve of her neck and opened his door. "It's okay,'' he said through gritted teeth. ''I just want to get on the road again. We probably shouldn't have stopped, anyway.''

His curt words sent her scurrying into the front seat. ''You're right,'' she said. ''Please forgive me—I didn't mean to forget about your father.''

He shrugged as he fastened his seat belt, feeling like a heel. He had a lot of nerve making her feel guilty when *he* had been the one lingering over his greasy cheeseburger, giving a nun the third degree about her sex life. That didn't exactly show the greatest concern for his father's welfare.

But now that he thought about it, he wanted nothing more than to get back to his dad. To show him his grandchild. Henry would be ecstatic.

What was more, the sooner he got this weekend over with, the sooner he and Sister Alison could part company. Given the way his hormones were reacting to her—a woman who had devoted her life to celibacy and holiness!—he was beginning to think their parting company would be a *very good* thing.

''Next stop, home,'' Ross said, turning the key in the ignition.

But the Jaguar didn't respond. Not with a click or even a sputter. ''I don't believe this!'' he muttered, attempting to turn over the engine again and again.

''I don't suppose you have AAA?'' Alison asked after several of his efforts failed.

He pumped the gas pedal. ''No.'' Almost 11 p.m. in a nonexistent town in West Texas, and the darn car wouldn't start. He flopped back in his seat. ''I suppose we'll have to try to find somewhere around here to get the car fixed.''

With dwindling hopes, both of them looked out at the empty darkness around them.

"YEP, YOU'VE GOT some kind of problem with this car," Earl Woodard announced.

"Earl knows all about cars," Darla informed them for the tenth time in the ten minutes that Earl's head had been under the Jaguar's hood.

Earl and Darla certainly looked like brother and sister. He even appeared to have come by the same straw-colored blond hair naturally—maybe Darla dyed her hair to match his.

Suppressing a sigh, Ross looked at Alison. "I told you we should have flown," she said.

He hadn't walloped a female since Kathy Robichaux in the second grade, but he was sorely tempted now. And maybe he would have, if she hadn't brought up an important idea. He turned to Earl. "Is there an airfield nearby?"

Earl blinked. "You mean, you want to fly?" He looked up at the dark starless sky as if he couldn't imagine such a thing.

"There's a landing strip," Darla interjected. "It's about thirty miles from here. But it don't have no planes there for rent. Except if you hire them in advance."

Which left them back where they started. Out in the middle of nowhere with no other transportation in sight. What if he didn't get back to his father in time? Strange, he'd always thought that having all the money in the world would rescue him from any difficulty. He never realized just how important a part dumb luck played in life. He would swap a million dollars for a little of that dumb stuff right this minute.

Alison looked sincerely contrite. "I'm sorry, Ross."

He shook his head. "Never mind."

"If'n I was you, I'd have the car towed over to Miller's garage," Earl said helpfully. "Jim Miller's a cousin of mine. He knows all about cars."

"Where is this garage?"

"In town."

"By your hotel?"

"No, it's in another town. Brody. I can hitch you up now and haul you out in the a.m."

In the morning! Ross felt clammy with panic. He couldn't wait that long. He'd already been away from his father too long—almost an entire day. He'd had to go to Dallas to scare up a grandchild, but waiting for a sick Jaguar to get fixed seemed an unnecessary delay.

"Look, this is an emergency," Ross said. "Isn't there a car-rental place around here?"

Earl nodded. "Sure. My cousin Dwayne owns one. It's over in Brody, too."

Ross felt his muscles go limp with relief. "Good, could you—"

"Dwayne opens up at 8 a.m."

What was he going to do? He eyed Earl's beat-up white pickup enviously, but on second thought doubted that the vehicle could take them to Brody, much less to his father's ranch, which was still at least two and a half hours away.

"Earl's got plenty of rooms over at the motel," Darla suggested. "Real reasonable prices, too."

As if money was an obstacle, Ross thought. He looked inside the car and saw his cell phone's light winking at him. "Excuse me," he told the others, ducking into the privacy of the defunct car's front seat.

Behind him, he heard the soft gurgly fusses coming from Felicity.

Humming a few soothing bars of "Jumpin' Jack Flash," he punched in the numbers for the hospital, but all the nurse on the intensive-care ward would tell him was that his father was sleeping.

He dialed the number for the ranch. After three rings Hannah, his father's housekeeper, answered, obviously having been roused from sleep. She informed Ross that late in the afternoon the doctors had performed an angioplasty on his father, the results of which would be back the next morning early. She assured him the doctor had told her that, although his father's status was critical, he had been given painkillers and was sleeping soundly.

When Ross hung up the phone, he felt slightly less panicked. He would have to wait until morning. What choice did he have?

He got out of the car and glanced apologetically at Alison, then looked back at Earl. "You say you can put us up in a room tonight?"

Chapter Four

Three grown-ups and a baby were a tight squeeze on the bench seat of Earl's pickup truck. Though the men protested that it was only a short trip to Earl's Motel, Felicity's guardian for the weekend, Alison, insisted that the baby's car seat take one of the precious seat-belted spaces. After battening down Felicity in the center seat, however, she was left with no alternative but squeezing herself into the nonexistent space between the car seat and Ross.

"You might as well sit in my lap," Ross suggested as they attempted to defy the law of physics and jam their bodies into the unmanageable space.

She sent him a disbelieving look. Despite their automotive difficulties, they were both still keyed up from their discussion of Alison's sex life. There was no doubt in her mind that he was attracted to her—or that the feeling was mutual. Going anywhere near his lap at this moment would just be playing with fire.

Brown eyes warred with blue in a standoff. Finally Ross relented. "Okay—I guess I could use a little fresh air. I'll climb into the back."

As Earl took the driver's seat, Ross got out and jumped into the bed of the truck, looking none too happy about doing so. When Alison glanced back at him, he was hunched in the corner, looking dejected and windblown.

Apparently Felicity wasn't any more pleased with the arrangement than Ross was. She fussed unhappily. Once she even whacked Earl on the forearm.

The man laughed. "That baby's a cute thing, but five'll get you ten she turns out to be a real hell-raiser."

Alison wasn't going to argue with that prediction. She smoothed down a soft curl of silky baby hair and silently sent up a prayer of gratitude that she wasn't going to be the one to have to deal with Felicity's terrible twos, elementary-school shenanigans and teenage rebellion.

As if in answer to her thoughts, Felicity sent up a wail.

"Doesn't anything quiet that kid down?" Earl asked.

"Music," Alison said quickly. "Does this car have a radio?"

"Heck, no. That broke sometime back in 'eighty-two." He smiled. "But, hey, you're in luck. I love to sing. Got a pretty good voice, too, my wives have always told me."

Before Alison could question just how many wives he'd had, Earl burst into a heartfelt full-throated rendering of "Desperado," the old Eagles song. Alison recognized the words, but the tune was hopelessly, if lovingly, mangled. The man might just as well have dragged a garden rake against the rusty metal of the truck's hood.

Felicity's gaze was riveted on Earl—her blue eyes open wide and lips parted in wonder. Probably in her short life her little ears had never experienced such complete lack of tunefulness.

Alison suppressed a smile but couldn't help glancing back at Ross, whose head was turned. He stared at the back window with equal parts humor and pain. By the time they drove into the dirt parking lot of Earl's Motel, which turned out to be a ten-room roadside affair, Alison was more than ready to get out of the truck.

"Say, you were right about that baby," Earl noted as he led the way into the small vinyl-paneled office of the motel. "She's got a real good ear for music." He thumbed through a book on the desk between them. "Now let's see..."

Alison hadn't noticed any other cars in the parking lot, so she doubted there were any other guests staying at the motel, but Earl made a show of picking out the very best room for them, anyway.

"I'll put you all in room six," he said. "I think you'll be really comfy there—it's got a TV and everything."

Ross smiled. "We won't have time for TV," he reminded Earl. "Since we'll be getting up early to get the car towed to Brody."

Earl snapped his fingers. "That's right. Don't you worry, either. I'll be up before the bugs to call my cousin. Jim'll have ya'll ready to go in no time." He tossed Alison the room key with a flourish.

She caught it, but as she felt the single piece of metal sink into her palm, her face heated with realization. One. One room. For three people!

"We need another room," she said.

Ross narrowed his eyes on her warningly. She didn't care. He might be paying the nuns of St. Felicity's handsomely for her services, but sleeping in a hotel room with a man she barely knew was *not* part of the bargain!

Earl was looking at her strangely. "Most couples just take one."

Alison cleared her throat, trying to think fast. "Yes, but you see, Ross snores. Terribly loud. It keeps the baby up. It just might keep *you* up, too," she warned him for good measure. "Better give Ross a room far, far from all of us."

"Well, now, I certainly would be glad to," Earl said, biting his lip as he thought through this new conundrum. "But we really only got three rooms here, on account of I had to hock some of the furniture last Christmas 'cause of some gambling debts."

"All we need is two," Alison told the man. She didn't look at Ross—she knew he would be annoyed. But what did he care? With all his money, he surely couldn't begrudge her the price of a room of her own.

Unless he'd had ideas about what might happen sharing one room…

Her face flamed and she held out her hand. "If you'll just give me the other key…"

Earl scratched his head. "Well, now, see, there's this little problem. 'Cause there was some roof damage, and there's a pretty hairy leak in one of the rooms. You know, it's gonna rain tonight…"

"I can swim," Alison told him.

"But there ain't a mattress in there."

That *was* a problem. "Then I'll take the other one."

"It ain't made up," Earl said.

Alison stamped her foot impatiently. "Are you telling me this hotel only has *one room?*"

"Alison..." Ross said warningly. He smiled at Earl. "We'll just take the one room."

"No, we will not," Alison insisted.

Earl looked from one to the other anxiously.

"Honeycakes," Ross said, "we need to get some sleep sometime between now and dawn. We don't have time to argue the issue or clean up a room."

Alison pursed her lips. "I'll sleep in the truck."

As Earl's eyes widened in surprise, Ross's narrowed to cool slits. "Aren't you going a bit overboard?"

"I don't think so!"

"Say..." Earl looked down and frowned.

Alison followed his gaze to where it was focused—on her left hand.

"Wait a minute," Earl said ominously. "Darla told me ya'll was married." He glared at Ross. "I'm a marryin' man myself. Don't want any hanky-panky going on in my motel."

Ross and Alison exchanged worried glances. Were they about to be kicked out of the motel—and by a man who had just referred offhandedly to his multiple wives?

Sleeping in a motel room with Ross wasn't something she wanted to do—but it beat hitchhiking to another motel or sleeping on the ground! And Ross was right. They did need to get some kind of rest before tomorrow or she wasn't sure how she would hold up when it came time to meet his father.

"Oh, dear," she piped up, thinking quickly. "You've just touched on a sore point. I, uh, had taken my ring off while I was showering the other day, but it fell off the soap dish and washed down the drain. We've called three plumbers and none has been able to retrieve it. I'm just sick about it, and Ross hasn't let me forget it either."

Earl looked relieved, albeit disturbed by the incompetence of plumbers in Dallas. "That's a doggone shame. Why, I've got a cousin in Luling who's a plumber, and I bet he wouldn't have any trouble fishing a little bitty ring out of a bathtub drain."

"I'm sure room eight will be fine," Ross said, hustling Alison toward the door. "Thank you for your help."

Alison nodded. "He really doesn't snore that badly!"

When Ross and Alison finally made it out of the office, he turned on her sharply. "What's the matter with you?"

"I barely know you!" she said. Then, to make it clear no hanky-panky would be allowed, she reminded him, "Besides, I'm a nun. Remember? I'm not used to sleeping in motel rooms with strangers."

"Don't worry, Sister Honeycakes," Ross replied, shlepping the lion's share of their luggage. "You're safe with me. I'm ready to turn in."

When they reached room eight, Alison opened the door and flipped on the light, illuminating a small space with a big problem. Both she and Ross drew in their breaths in surprise. Centered in the middle of the tiny, brown-shag-carpeted space, was a double bed.

One double bed.

"We can't both sleep in that!" she exclaimed, scanning Ross's six-foot frame. She doubted he would be very comfortable in a bed that small all by himself. With two of them it would be a squeeze—a very intimate squeeze.

"But we'll have to," Ross told her grimly. "And Felicity, too."

Felicity was the least of her worries! Alison didn't know if she could explain this properly, but wedged up against Ross all night, she was going to find it hard to get forty winks. Or even four winks.

Holding the baby fast, she faced Ross, fully prepared to march back to the motel office and talk to Earl. "We'll just have to insist on the other room. I can sleep without sheets, or with a few drips on me during the night."

"And tell him your story about losing your wedding ring was just an elaborate lie?"

"Well..." She bit her lip, searching for a way to couch the situation that Earl would accept. "If I just explained the truth, that I'm a nun, and that your father..." She shrugged. "It's not that far-fetched."

Ross rolled his eyes. "I'm not going to risk you getting us run out of a two-person town." He pried Felicity out of Alison's rigid arms. "Don't worry. I'm not a wolf."

"Well, yes, I know." She felt silly, but couldn't help glancing anxiously at the bed again. "It's just the bed's so small."

He followed her gaze and then stared at her, a grin spreading across his mouth that was a little wolfish at that, despite his protests. "Maybe it's yourself you don't trust, Sister."

"Don't be ridiculous!" she exclaimed. "Or impertinent!" There. Nuns in school had always used that word when she'd sassed back.

Unfortunately it didn't seem to be having the desired effect on Ross. He merely stood in the center of the room still smiling at her. A hot flush crept up her

neck and into her cheeks. Without Felicity to hold in front of her like a shield, she fiddled awkwardly with her hands.

"I…I was just thinking about…comfort," she protested.

"As in, we'll be too close for comfort?" He chuckled, then turned and placed Felicity in the center of the bed, constructing a playpen type barricade around the baby with pillows. "You can rest easy, Alison. Making a pass at a nun would require more energy than I could muster right now, I'm afraid."

"I'm so glad to hear that." Alison shifted uncomfortably, not sure how much solace to take from his words. She reached for her suitcase and hauled it onto an orange chair next to the television in the corner. Did he mean that if he had more energy, he *would* make a pass at her?

She glanced back at him suspiciously—but what she saw made her mouth go dry. While she was playing with Felicity in her pillow fortress, Ross had casually stripped off his shirt and sat there, with all his pectoral assets laid bare for the world to see. Alison attempted to gulp down some air. Although she had sworn off being attracted to sheer physical beauty just the same as she had sworn off filthy-rich men, she had to admit the man was a fine specimen. His muscular shoulders and arms weren't too overdone, and his skin was tanned the same hue of bronze as the rest of him. A light dusting of hair splayed across his chest and tapered down his flat, washboard abs.

Alison, who was staring at the point where the trail of hair disappeared from view, realized what she was doing, then looked away quickly.

I'm a nun, I'm a nun…

And I have the hots for my bedmate. Great.

Could things get much worse?

Huffing out a breath that was ninety percent sexual frustration, she popped the locks on her suitcase. Because Sister Joan had jam-packed the bag with clothes while Alison was busy dressing, the top of the suitcase practically clipped her on the jaw as it flew open. Alison jumped back, eyed the mound of garments that had created the explosion, then groaned. There, on the top layer of clothes, lay a flimsy, practically see-through purple lace nightgown. She was definitely *not* wearing that to bed with Ross!

''Is something wrong?'' Ross asked, watching her curiously.

Barely able to take her eyes off her nightmare potpourri of skimpy lingerie, she barked, ''No, nothing!''

She dug down deeper, trying to find something a little safer. Unfortunately the longer she looked, the more frantic she became. Sister Joan had discarded all the practical items of clothing she had so carefully picked, replacing them, apparently, with anything frilly and sheer that caught her eye. None of her oversize T-shirts had even made it in. At least she could have worn one of those at night without being too embarrassed.

She sent out a silent hex on Sister Joan. When she got back to Dallas, she swore she would get even with that nun.

But what was she going to do now?

She could feel Ross's gaze boring into her back as she stood in a trance in front of her clothes. ''I'm about ready to turn in, aren't you?'' he asked.

She slapped the top of her suitcase closed and turned quickly. No way did she wanting him peeking at its contents. Of course, he would see the contents when she finally had to *wear* them. Unless…

Eyeing the bathroom door, she gathered up the suitcase, holding it in front of her chest like an armor plate, and sprinted for sanctuary. "I'll be right out!" she called, shutting the bathroom door and throwing the lock.

WHAT THE HECK was she doing in there?

For about the hundredth time, Ross flicked an annoyed gaze at the firmly closed bathroom door. Alison had been locked in there forever, yet the shower had quit running more than half an hour ago. The distinct feeling that she was waiting for him to disappear, or at least fall asleep, began to creep into his mind.

Well, if she did want him to drop off, he would have no trouble obliging her. He rolled a newly diapered but still cranky Felicity a little farther toward the center of the bed and climbed in, bone-weary. He'd been telling Alison the truth when he said that he had no energy for making a pass at a woman. What with worry about his father and running around Dallas trying to find a baby and then the calamity with the car, he was ready to drop in his tracks. For the moment it didn't even matter that his tracks had led him to a small motel-room bed with a very attractive woman he couldn't lay a finger on.

Ross leaned over to the bedside table and turned off the lamp. Then he flopped against the pillows and closed his eyes.

After a few moments he began to hear stirrings of life again in the bathroom. Finally the sound of the lock being unbolted and the doorknob's subtle rattling indicated that Alison was ready to come out.

He lifted his lids a fraction, squinting through the darkness just in time to see a streak of black shoot across the room and dive under the covers. The bed shifted as Alison positioned herself on the opposite edge of the mattress.

But in his mind's eye Ross was still seeing that black streak. That *revealing* black streak. Even though she had been little more than a blur, Ross knew what he'd seen. Pale skin barely covered by some sort of dark filmy material. Long, exposed legs. Luscious curves.

He blinked, then turned to look at Alison, who was little more than two eyes peering at him in the darkness. The sheets were pulled up to her chin. "I thought you were asleep," she said testily.

He'd been sleepy, that was true. Hard to believe. Now every particle of his being was wide-awake.

"What are you staring at?" she asked.

He swallowed past the dry lump that had materialized in his throat. "Nothing."

Between them Felicity beat her fist against a pillow.

Alison sucked in a breath and bolted upright to a sitting position. "Felicity!" she cried, as if she'd forgotten all about her. "We've got to get you ready for bed."

"I did that," Ross informed her.

Despite the darkness, he could see her eyes widen in disbelief. "You? How?"

"Well, it wasn't easy, seeing as the bathroom was in use, but I did the best I could."

"But she'll need a new diaper..."

"I did that," Ross repeated.

Heedless of his words, Alison pivoted and flicked on the light. She already had the baby's Winnie the

Pooh sleeper unsnapped when she saw that he'd been telling the truth. The baby had a fresh diaper and smelled unmistakably of baby wipes and talc. Alison carefully inspected his handiwork with something approaching awe, while Felicity fussed unhappily at her intrusion.

"You *did* change her," she said in a low, almost admiring voice. "Not bad. But how...?"

Even in the nineties, women still thought they had cornered the market in baby care. "Those diapers come with instructions now, you know," he said.

She frowned and smoothed Felicity's unruly curls, which was a lot simpler than soothing her unruly temper. "I see."

Unfortunately he could see, too. While Alison had been checking out his diapering skills, the covers that had been pulled to her chin had fallen to her waist, giving Ross his first clear look at the thin, barely opaque silky black material covering her. The nightie was a mere wisp of a thing, hugging her full breasts loosely but revealingly, and held up only by two spaghetti-thin straps. The dark material made her light skin seem even fairer, almost creamy in contrast. And though she was soft and curvaceous in all the right places, her jutting collarbones and slim arms made her appear touchingly delicate.

He knew he was gawking, but he couldn't seem to help himself. When he looked into her brown eyes, the familiar wariness was there.

He took a deep breath and tried to marshal his senses. "Is this outfit standard-issue convent wear?"

She pulled up the covers defensively. But Ross wouldn't forget what she was hiding anytime soon.

Alison had a body men dreamed of. That *he* dreamed of.

"Th-the nuns in our order are allowed certain…liberties in what we choose to wear," she stammered.

"Really?" He cocked his head. "Seems to me you're choosing clothes that allow certain liberties."

Those covers were hoisted up another inch or two. "Just because I have a weakness for fine things doesn't mean I have a weakness for you, Mr. Templeton. Are you forgetting who I am? *What* I am?"

If only I could! he thought with an inward groan. He briefly remembered the Little Angels' receptionist, Dee. Multiple earrings or no, he wished he could have brought her, instead of Sister Alison. Maybe if he'd offered her enough money, she would have skipped her sister's wedding. He hadn't been the least bit attracted to Dee. And in the unlikely event that he had developed a weakness for pierced eyebrows, at least *she* wasn't a nun!

"It's not that *I've* forgotten you're a nun—it's that I'm beginning to wonder whether *you* have," he said, his irritation evident in his voice.

"I haven't," she said firmly. "I just…packed unwisely."

He tilted his head and looked her straight in the eye. "And yet you knew you would be coming here with me." An idea that had been rolling around in the dusty corners of his consciousness was beginning to seem more plausible.

Could "Sister" Alison be a phony? He didn't know what would cause her to lie about something like that…but she certainly didn't present a very convincing case of a woman who'd taken a vow of celibacy.

Then again, if she were just pretending to be a nun, why would she be doing such a lousy job of it?

"Naturally I couldn't have foreseen that we would be…in such close quarters."

"So I assume that back at St. Felicity's you have nightgowns that aren't so revealing?" he asked.

"Y-yes, of course," she said. "Big flannel nightgowns with long sleeves and high necks. Actually I prefer those. I really do. But you told me to pack normal things. I *am* supposed to be your girlfriend, you know."

He measured her response doubtfully—especially the anxious little tremor in her voice. She was definitely hiding something.

"How was I to know that we would be sharing a bed?" she continued.

She wouldn't have, of course. But there was something that still bothered him. Something she hadn't been able to explain to his satisfaction.

Even if she was just pretending to be his girlfriend, she had certainly rounded up all the appropriate props quickly. *What kind of nun had a weakness for skimpy black nighties?*

Maybe the same kind of nun who liked flame red nail polish.

And could suck down beer like it was mother's milk.

Alison squirmed uncomfortably under his gaze. "Anyway," she said prissily, "it's just plain silly to sit around talking about my nightwear when we should be sleeping. It's after midnight."

And Earl had said he'd be up with the bugs. No telling what that meant.

"Okay," Ross said, giving her a final glance. She was right about their needing to sleep. "Night."

"Good night."

In unison, both of them tossed onto their sides so that they faced away from each other. Alison turned off the light, plunging the room into darkness. And silence. Ross was amazed at how loud his own breathing seemed to his ears. He listened carefully to see if Alison had dropped off to sleep yet, but could only make out Felicity's coughing sputters. And just on the other side of Felicity, he thought with dismay, lay Alison, in that little black nightgown, trying to pretend she was dozing.

Good heavens! Maybe Alison was right—his ethics were definitely on a downward slide. First he'd decided to rent a baby so he could lie to his father. That was troubling enough, even though he had a good reason for doing it. But now he was falling for a nun and trying to rationalize it by clinging to the unlikely hope that she wasn't *really* a nun. If one of his buddies had confessed this sad tale to him, Ross would have counseled the pathetic creature to seek professional help.

His thoughts and the silence around them were suddenly interrupted by a terrible piercing howl.

The light snapped on, and both Ross and Alison turned, bleary-eyed, to see a beet red Felicity, her face scrunched in some unintelligible but very powerful emotion.

"What's the matter with her now?" Ross asked, after a hug and an offer of a pacifier failed to soothe her. He felt irritated by his inability to help her. This evening he'd thought he'd made some progress in bonding with Felicity, but apparently not as much as he'd hoped. After looking into her face for an answer, he lifted her onto his chest and patted her gently on her back.

Alison leaned over. ''Did you do something to her?''

''Of course not,'' Ross said, offended, bouncing the baby gently. The curt tone he'd used with Alison only seemed to upset Felicity more.

''She just ate,'' Alison said, ticking off the list of possibilities, ''and she's got a dry diaper. What else could she want?''

They lay contemplating their red-faced charge in bewilderment.

After a few unproductive moments Ross turned to Alison. ''We might as well try plan A,'' he told her.

She shrugged, nodded and took a breath. After a few bars of ''Mr. Tambourine Man,'' Ross joined in, faintly. He leaned back against the pillows, hoping his own prone position would coax Felicity to sleep. ''Mr. Tambourine Man'' had never been one of his favorites, but it did have a sort of lullaby quality to it. Or at least it did as sung with Alison's warm alto voice. She knew the words much better than he did, so he had to drop off after the first verse, after which she continued solo.

And after which, his eyelids drooping heavily, Ross nodded off as quickly as Felicity.

SOMETHING WAS NUZZLING her ear. Alison flicked her head and smiled, nestling a little closer into the warmth of the bed around her. Something was playing with a lock of hair that had fallen over her face, and she tilted her head up, like a blind burrowing mole, sniffing the air to test it.

It smelled good. Male.

Wriggling closer and wrapping her arms around the object that she had mistakenly assumed was a pillow, Alison tilted her head and found herself enveloped in a sensual kiss. Of the toe-curling variety. Warm lips covered hers. Strong hands at her back drew her close. Their tongues entwined and she moaned.

It had been so long since she had been coaxed out of a deep sleep this way. It felt so wonderful, so right, snuggled close to a body that seemed to fit hers like a glove. She undulated a little closer, trying to fill in every possible gap of space between them.

Then, in the twilight of half sleep, she felt her hand hit something completely unfamiliar—at least in her experience. Then her hand latched on to what felt like a tiny foot.

Felicity let out an indignant howl.

Alison bolted upright—and found herself straddling Ross's body. His very *aroused body.*

She looked at his face. Even in the dark she could see the whites of his eyes, which must have been as bugged out in surprise as her own were.

With a yelp of dismay that more than matched Felicity's, Alison rocketed off the bed like a missile. Ross shot up, too; only he landed on the other side of the bed and flipped on the lamp.

Alison blinked against the bright light and then, remembering her lack of covering, crossed one of her arms over her chest. As if that would hide anything.

Ross, almost speechless, pointed at her. "You..."

She shook her head, wishing he would put his finger down. Wishing Sister Joan hadn't unpacked her robe. "It wasn't what you're thinking," she said.

"You were kissing me."

"Yes, but—"

He shook his head. "That *wasn't* a nun's kiss, Alison."

"Oh, really? How many nuns have you kissed?"

"What's your last name?" His voice was stony.

"Why?"

"What is it?" he repeated, unrelenting.

"Bennett," she said, seeing he wasn't going to give in. "Why?"

"Because the minute I get home, I'm going to do a Lexus-Nexus search on you, lady. I don't know what I'll come up with, but I can bet one thing. I won't find out that you're a sister at St. Felicity's."

A search. Her heart went cold. She'd forgotten. Rich people had their ways, and more often than not, their ways included methods meant to protect their interests. Wes, too, had run a background check on her. When that had failed to turn up anything provocative, he'd still made her sign a prenuptial agreement. Just for good measure.

And then he'd dumped her, anyway. Too bad she hadn't forced *him* to sign an agreement saying he'd show up for their wedding!

Although Wes's behavior was unrelated, technically, to what Ross was saying, for all the anger building inside her she might have been facing Wes himself. And that thought put her in a suitably grim mood to face up to the truth. After Ross's statement that he was going to run a background check, she would lay money that she'd no longer have to worry about a weakness for him. The man was anathema to her.

"You're right," she confessed, proud of the lack of contrition in her voice. "You wouldn't find out that I'm a nun."

He blinked, obviously caught off guard by her honesty. His hand, still gesturing at her in a point, collapsed to his side. "Why not?"

She pursed her lips. "Because I'm not a nun." Shrugging, she admitted, "I lied to you."

There was a moment of silence as waves of several different emotions played across Ross's face. Shock. Relief. Even pleasure. Then, as understanding dawned and she could see him mentally tallying all the falsehoods she'd told him, he stamped his foot. "I knew it!"

"I lied because you seemed exactly the type of high-handed arrogant male I've made a concerted effort to avoid. If I was going to be forced to travel with you, I wanted something that would keep us at a distance."

He crossed his arms, looking smug. "Didn't seem to work so well, did it, Sister?"

The last word came out in a sardonic tone that rankled. "No, it didn't. But I might have known that, to a man like you, who would lie to his own father, the idea of respecting someone else's vows would be merely a small obstacle to overcome."

Shade by shade, his face mutated from Maui tan to lobster red, which contrasted sharply with the white T-shirt he wore over a pair of short plaid pajama bottoms. Alison struggled to keep her mind off his attractively muscled thighs and focused on the fact that he looked like he just might pop with rage.

"As far as I'm concerned, you've lost all right to preach to anyone about ethics," he said. "At least what I'm doing is for my father's sake."

The baby cried and Ross reached down and lifted her to his chest, patting her gently on the back like an old pro as he set about the task of finding her bottle.

Alison was amazed at the transformation. Just yesterday the man had eyed the little girl as if she were an exotic animal in a pet-store window. Now, with little ado, he was acting as if he really *were* the father he was going to pretend to be.

Alison had been around little kids for a long time. She'd seen commercials being made with hunks and angelic kids frolicking together, meant to seduce women to buy everything from minivans to air freshener. But until just this moment, she'd never been moved by such an image herself. Before seeing Ross and Felicity together, she'd never really known how sexy a man holding a baby could be.

Sexy and infuriating.

''What are you staring at?'' Ross asked, his voice testy.

You. Perfection. ''Nothing.'' She'd die before she admitted how attracted she still was to him.

He looked around the room. ''Start packing. It's five o'clock. Maybe Earl's gotten in touch with that cousin of his already.''

And maybe Ross just wanted to get out of the motel room as quickly as possible. She couldn't blame him. She wasn't much interested in lingering herself. ''All right,'' she said, turning to her suitcase.

She felt more ridiculous than ever, traipsing around in her Victoria's Secret sale-catalog special. The faded jeans peeking out of the corner of her bag looked mighty appealing. She pulled them out, along with a short-sleeved yellow shirt. As she headed for the bathroom, Ross stopped her.

''I just want you to know that whatever happened this morning between us will not be repeated.''

''I know that,'' Alison assured him.

"I have a lot of responsibilities on my plate," he went on, adjusting the angle he was holding Felicity's bottle. "I'm not looking for a relationship right now. That's why the only kind of wife and kid I wanted were the kind I could rent. What happened this morning was a mistake."

"Yes, it was," she said. *High-handed arrogant man,* she thought. Now that he'd discovered she was available, he was putting up all sorts of barriers.

"So you see, you have nothing to fear from me. The last thing I want is real involvement," he finished.

Which, apparently, was a whole different matter from a quick fling with a woman he assumed was a nun.

She didn't know why, but his going on and on about how he didn't want to get involved with her smacked of insult. It shouldn't have, since she felt precisely the same way. But he made it sound as if the news that he wasn't wife-hunting was going to crush her.

She held her clothes more closely to her and nodded in the most businesslike way one could in a see-through nightie. "And you can rest assured, Ross, that the last thing I care to do is jump into another bed with you."

And with that, she turned and fled into the bathroom, buoyed up a little by the clenched-jaw affront she saw on his face just before she closed the door.

Chapter Five

Earl spat, sending an arc of Red Man chewing tobacco flying through the air. It landed on the ground with a wet ominous plop. "I got bad news for you folks," he told Ross and Alison, who were standing outside the office door with Felicity and all their belongings, ready to go. He seemed completely oblivious to the thick tension between them.

Ross could think of little else. Since flitting out of the room to change clothes, Alison had barely spoken two words to him. He didn't know why her silence disturbed him so. After all, he was just using her for his own ends.

But now it seemed those ends were unraveling. He looked into Earl's eyes and felt his heart sink.

"I called cousin Jim just a minute ago, and his wife says he'd done gone out of town."

"Out of town?" Alison echoed.

"How far?" Ross asked. Maybe, if they could get him back—

"Houston," Earl replied, cutting short that hope.

"There must be someone else around who works on cars."

Earl shook his head. "Oh, sure, there're plenty of

guys who'll work on your car...if you're drivin' a Chevy or a Ford, or even a Subaru. But around here we get more raindrops than automobiles like the kind you drive."

Ross thought he detected a hint of smugness in Alison's face and steeled himself against the anger building in him. There was no time to argue with her now.

"Well, what do you recommend?" Ross asked. "We're in a hurry. Didn't you say you had another relative who owned a car-rental business?"

The man scratched his head in thought. "Oh, sure. But he don't open till eight."

It was now almost six.

"Heck, you won't even be able to get breakfast at Darla's till seven."

Ross bit his lip and gazed in frustration out at the emptiness around them. He was accustomed to this landscape. He'd grown up in it. But it had never looked as bleak as now.

Then his eyes settled on Earl's banged-up, barely-holding-together dinosaur of a pickup. Suddenly it seemed like the only way out.

"How much for your truck?" he asked Earl.

Earl looked stunned. "You want to *buy* my truck?"

"Ross, surely..."

Ross felt Alison tugging at his shirtsleeve and responded, "No, I want to rent it. I'll pay you whatever you want. I have to get home to see my father," he said, appealing to the man's emotions. "He's dying."

Earl stared at him, obviously moved. Then he looked at his pickup, his old friend. "Gosh...it'd be hard to put a price on her...."

"Name one," Ross said impatiently. When Earl

proved too slow at computation, he pulled out his wallet, suggesting, "I'll give you three hundred dollars."

The man looked dumbfounded. Ross pulled another couple of Franklins out of his wallet and shoved them into Earl's hands. "Five hundred. And I'll bring it back as soon as I can."

Earl gripped his windfall in his hands and swallowed. "Sure thing. Take your time." Quickly, maybe before Ross could change his mind, he fished the key out of his pocket and handed it to him. "You gotta be careful 'cause the gas gauge doesn't exactly work, and I should warn you, the gear sticks a little in second and fourth. Maybe a little in third, too."

Ross and Alison loaded their things into the truck while Earl regaled them with information about the truck's shortcomings. He also said he had a cousin with a tow truck who would take the Jaguar to Jim's to be worked on when that particular cousin returned from his sojourn in Houston.

Ross was beginning to feel better for the first time that day.

Actually that wasn't entirely the truth. He'd felt a lot better the moment he learned he wasn't lusting after a nun. The relief had been short-lived, however. Alison took great pains to let him know that she didn't appreciate him lusting after her—even if she *was* wearing a skimpy yellow blouse and faded jeans that hugged her sexy bottom like a glove.

He made himself busy strapping the car seat into the center of the truck's cab. At least he and Alison still had Felicity to take their minds off each other. And of course, he had his father to worry about. Once they got on the road, he needed to call Hannah again and get a status report.

But inevitably his gaze strayed back to Alison, especially when they were finally loaded up and she climbed into the pickup next to him. The grimy cab suddenly became an intimate space. Better smelling, too. Alison's hint of perfume did valiant battle with the upholstery's long-ingrained stench of tobacco juice.

Face it. It would take a miracle to make him forget the way she'd felt in his arms that morning, kissing him. For him it was like awakening in heaven. She was as soft and warm and delightful as all his guilty fantasies of the day before had convinced him she would be. But of course he'd known immediately she wasn't a nun—it would have been a travesty of nature.

Alison reached back to tuck her hair into an elastic doodad and then rolled down the window a little bit, letting in some badly needed air.

Ross shook thoughts of kissing out of his head and sent up a little prayer to the transmission gods as he pushed in the clutch and turned the key. Luckily the engine turned over on the first try and sputtered happily.

Earl waved to them as they pulled out.

"How far is it to your ranch?" Alison asked.

"Two and a half hours, I guess," Ross said, stepping on the gas. "But I intend to make it in two."

Alison appeared alarmed to be barreling down the road at a speed that practically made the old truck shudder. Yet she said nothing, which was a good thing. Maybe she sensed he might just explode if she did.

They drove in silence.

Alison sighed. Ross flicked an annoyed gaze at her, then felt even more annoyed when he found his gaze latched on to her breasts pushing against the yellow fabric of her shirt.

"What's the matter?" she asked briskly.

He returned his gaze to the road, startled and tense. "Nothing."

She crossed her arms.

Damn, Ross thought. Why was he still attracted to her?

Then again, why wouldn't he be? Nothing had changed, except that he'd learned she was available. That is, if she *was* available...

He drove on for as long as he could withstand the curiosity building inside him. Which wasn't long.

Finally he heard himself blurt, "So this guy..."

Her head flicked toward him. "What guy?"

He shrugged, feigning casualness. Trying not to look into those melting brown eyes of hers. "You know, the one you were telling me about. The man you almost married." *Wes,* he could have spit out—but he didn't want her to know exactly how much that name had stuck in his craw.

She said nothing for a moment, then asked, "What about him?"

"Were you telling me the truth about the wedding?"

Unintentionally his tone sounded as if he thought he couldn't trust her word on anything anymore, which, despite her previous fib, he suspected wasn't true. Alison took offense.

"If you want the whole truth, Your Honor, he stood me up at the altar."

"You mean, on your wedding day?" That was brutal!

She nodded. "So you can see why I'm not so enthusiastic about pursuing relationships. Plus, I have my business—that keeps me busy..."

When her voice trailed off, Ross felt the first crack of ice melting in his heart. "Running a business can be a consuming thing. I have this new project in Switzerland—it means almost as much as a romance to me."

She swung her head to look at him again. "Then you don't have a significant other right now?"

"No," he said, then added quickly, "There was someone once. A woman named Cara. But we weren't compatible."

He couldn't say why, but he didn't want Alison to think that he'd never had a serious relationship before—that he had no depth. He wasn't sure what he wanted Alison *to* think. All he knew was that his feelings for her seemed to be getting more confusing than ever now that he knew she wasn't a nun.

And was definitely available.

Maybe stress was driving his hormones out of control. He needed to get back to his father, he thought, pushing down the accelerator another notch or so.

Alison craned her neck to see the speedometer. "You don't want to go too fast," she told him. "Getting stopped by a cop won't save us any time."

"Spoken just like Sister Alison," Ross said, enjoying the way she bristled. Before she could respond, he assured her with a little swagger in his voice, "I'm not going to get a ticket. I've been driving these roads all my life—know 'em like the back of my hand. I haven't been stopped since I was sixteen."

She frowned, then shrugged. "It's your license."

The words still had a prissy ring to them, which pleased Ross in a backhand sort of way. It was a lot easier on his nerves to be annoyed with Alison than to lust after her.

"OKAY, BUD, LET'S SEE your license."

At least Ross had the decency to send a sheepish sideways glance at Alison so she could gloat a little. She didn't feel too self-satisfied, however. Despite her animosity toward the man, she understood what the delay was costing him. More than anything, Ross wanted to get home, but they'd only been driving about thirty minutes when they'd seen the flashing lights of the cop car.

Ross fished his license out of his wallet and handed it to the officer. "I know I was speeding, sir, but if you'd just let me ex—"

"Uh-huh," the cop said, looking skeptically at the license, then at Ross. He glanced at Felicity, then at Alison. "Who are your passengers?"

Ross looked at Alison, too, a hint of doubt in his eyes. "This is, uh, my wife and child."

"Names?"

"My name is Alison Bennett," Alison said. "And this is Felicity."

The cop, whose badge said Teel, stared unsmilingly at her through his sunglasses, which were the silvery reflective kind that made the policeman look like a bug. In fact, the longer he gaped at her, the more Alison felt like a bug herself.

"Your name's Bennett and his name's Templeton," Officer Teel observed.

A clammy sweat broke out on Ross's brow. "You know these liberated women," he said with an uncertain laugh.

"Uh-huh." The officer wrote something down on a

pad, then looked up, all business again. "Did you realize that your inspection sticker's out of date, Mr. Templeton?"

Ross looked at the little sticker on the bottom left corner of the window. It had been expired for three months in fact. "Well, you see, it's a funny thing about this truck..."

The cop's lips thinned visibly. "You better show me your insurance papers, Mr. Templeton."

Ross flipped open the glove compartment in front of Alison and pulled out a wad of things—including a travel pack of Kleenex, a receipt for a new faucet, several yellowed empty Red Man pouches and, finally, the insurance for the truck.

At the discovery Ross began to look relieved, but Alison could tell that he remembered a key problem with their situation at the same time she did: the insurance was in Earl's name.

"I think I should tell you," Ross said as he handed over the papers, "this truck isn't ours, exactly."

"That's what I thought," Teel said, looking at the insurance form. "You folks better get out and come with me."

"With you?" Ross repeated, aghast. "Where?"

"Down to the station," the man said curtly. "You're driving a stolen vehicle."

Ross barked out a laugh, but Alison had an uneasy feeling. This cop wasn't in a joking mood. She poked Ross warningly in the ribs as he replied, "But that's ridiculous. We just rented it from the man this morning. Thirty minutes ago."

"Rented it," the cop repeated, shaking his head. "Right."

Alison looked at Ross and he sucked in a breath.

"You don't mean to say you think *we* stole the truck, do you?"

The cop finally smiled. "You didn't think I meant Earl stole it, did you?"

"Well, yes."

"Mister, Earl Woodard's my cousin. And I happen to know he's owned this old bus for twenty years. He wouldn't sell, rent or trade it for gold."

"He rented it to me for five hundred dollars," Ross said. "You see, my father is very ill—"

"Uh-huh," the cop said skeptically.

"You have to believe me," Ross pleaded.

"You have a receipt?"

"No—of course not."

"It was just a friendly transaction," Alison explained.

"Uh-huh." The cop nodded. "How long you two known Earl?"

Ross swallowed. "Well, just one night, but..."

The cop donned an officious you're-under-arrest demeanor. "Step out of the car, sir."

THE COUNTY JAIL was half-empty, but that didn't make being there any more pleasant to Ross. The place had the stench of stale cigarettes, old winos and unwashed bodies.

It sounded like Felicity's crying.

There were other sounds when he and Alison and Felicity had been led to their cell, which abutted the drunk tank on one side and a more felonious-looking cohort on the other. But now the snores, the colorful conversations about previous arrests, the card games and the shouted curses aimed at the policemen in the next room were all drowned out by the wails of one single baby. Ross had to admit, in the spare institutional setting, her cries echoed lustily in all directions.

Grown men stared at the baby, unnerved. Even the cops from the next room braved the shouted curses to come stare in awe at the little body who could create such a ruckus.

Alison looked like she wanted to kill. Not the baby. Not even Officer Teel. Ross.

"I told you not to speed," she said miserably.

He tried not to take her barb to heart. After all, he had landed them in a pretty unpleasant place. "Could I have foreseen this?"

"No, but once it happened you might have asked to call a lawyer or at least Earl Woodard. But no, who did you want to call to get us out of this fix? Your nanny! No wonder the officer refused to let you use the phone."

Ross puffed up in offense. "Hannah is my father's housekeeper," he said defensively, then added in a lower voice, "It's been years since she's been my nanny."

"I knew better," Alison said. "I knew better than to come on a fool's mission with a spoiled rich man."

"Will you stop calling me that?" Ross said. Not that he'd ever spent much time in jails, but he'd heard they made some people defiant and others crumble. Alison was apparently a crumbler. "I'll have you know I've worked like a slave since I finished Yale."

She lifted her big brown eyes to the heavens for patience, then turned them back on him. "How long do you think it will be before they track down Earl Woodard?" she asked. "How long do you think they'll keep us here for a lousy speeding ticket and an expired inspection sticker?"

"I believe we're really here because we're suspicious characters," Ross reminded her.

"You'd think after being a law-abiding citizen all my life I'd at least get credit for looking like one," she grumbled.

It was all he could do not to give her a lingering once-over. She looked so gorgeous—even in her orange jail scrub suit and mismatched flip-flops. He wanted to kiss the worried frown from her face.

"Don't worry, we'll get out of here."

Surprised, apparently, by his kindly tone, Alison tilted her head and glanced up at him. "Oh, Ross, I'm so selfish. I know you want out of here even more than I do."

Her change of attitude encouraged him. They had problems galore. The situation would be a little better, however, if they at least weren't hostile toward each other.

Felicity let out an especially lusty howl that made even some of the hardest-looking of their jail mates cover their ears and rock back and forth. Alison, who was more accustomed to the cries, merely winced and tried futilely to calm the baby.

"How?" she asked. "How are we going to get out? We can hardly make a jailbreak with a crying baby in tow."

Ross smiled and reached down into Felicity's car seat, which the sheriff had allowed them to bring in with them. "Voilà!"

He produced his cell phone and pressed the call button. Alison gaped at him, astonished. "How did you get that thing in here?"

"I sneaked it into the car seat before I got out of the car."

She hopped up. ''How wonderful!''

''I figured they wouldn't frisk Felicity,'' he explained, pleased to be regaining some of Alison's esteem.

She beamed at him as if he was some sort of hero.

''Hey, buddy,'' a drunken little man in the next cell called out, ''can I borrow that when you're through? I gotta call my wife and tell her I won't make it home for dinner.''

Several of his fellow inebriates expressed a similar desire. Luckily Felicity let out another wail, drowning out their requests. He didn't want the cops confiscating his one link to the outside world.

''Who are you calling?'' Alison asked.

''I'm calling the hospital, trying to get Hannah. She can tell me how my father's doing and get hold of a lawyer for us.''

Alison nodded, more agreeable to his calling the housekeeper now that he had come through with a phone.

He dialed the number to the hospital. After being routed through several different stations, he finally reached the nurse at the intensive-care unit.

''Hello, I'm calling to ask how Henry Templeton is doing. I'm his son.''

''I'm sorry,'' the nurse said. ''We can't give information about patients' health over the phone, sir.''

Ross gritted his teeth. ''Is my father still in intensive care?''

The nurse hesitated. ''Mr. Templeton, your father is being taken home this morning.''

''Taken home?''

''Yes, sir.''

Ross felt the blood drain out of his face. ''Thank

you,'' he said after the nurse stonewalled him on the particulars. ''Dad's going home,'' he told Alison.

She smiled. ''Congratulations,'' she said. ''That's good news.''

He couldn't share in her chirpiness. Instead, he punched in the numbers for his father's home. He needed to talk to Hannah. What the heck was going on here?

The phone rang and rang. No answer. No answering machine of course. His father didn't believe in them, except for business.

Alison touched his arm.

''Ross, what's the matter?''

''What if it's not good news?'' he asked. ''What if it's bad news?''

''How could it be bad? He's going home.''

Ross tried not to panic. Alison could be right. It might not be as bad as he feared. Then again…

''You don't understand,'' he said. ''Just yesterday Dad was in terrible pain. He'd had a heart attack. You wouldn't believe the number of tubes they had in him. And now, going home so suddenly…''

Her brow furrowed. ''What are you afraid of, Ross?''

''Well…'' He swallowed, then mumbled in a rush, ''Dad always said he didn't want to die in a hospital.''

Alison paled. ''Oh, Ross…''

He had to get out of there, had to get to his father. So much time had been wasted already. He'd been trying to do something good—to make his father happy one last time. Now he wondered if he hadn't squandered the last precious moments he could have spent with his dad.

As if in agreement with his gloomy mood, Felicity

let out a howl that rattled the concrete walls. A man in the next cell, a guy who had previously been bragging about his lengthy rap sheet, scowled through the bars. "Can't you tell that kid to shut up?"

Ross stiffened. He was in no mood to be hassled by a thug. "Yeah, I guess I could," he said, eyeing the man coldly.

"Ross..." Alison warned under her breath. "That's the one they've been calling Razor."

Ross knew he was being foolhardy, but he didn't care. It had been a helluva day, and it wasn't even 8 a.m. yet. "You got a problem?" he asked Razor.

"Yeah," the man said, standing and strutting up to the bars that connected their cells. When he gripped the bars, the muscles in his arms bulged threateningly. One set of biceps bore a Harley-Davidson insignia. On the other was a bleeding snake. "I got a problem. With you, Mr. Country Club."

"Yeah?" Ross mirrored the man's movements. "I got a problem with lowlifes taking out their anger on little kids."

"Fine. I'd rather take it out on you. Why're you even in here, Country Club? None of the rest of us get to have a phone, a woman or a screaming kid in our cells."

"Maybe because even the cops don't think you're worth it."

"Ross..."

Razor looked mad enough to spit nails. "I'm gonna get you, Country Club. When you gettin' outta here?"

"Sooner than you, Mr. Bic Shaver."

Fluttering nervously, Alison stepped up to the bars separating the two men. "I'm sorry our baby caused you discomfort, Mr. Razor,'' she said ingratiatingly. ''But you see, the atmosphere in here disturbs her.''

Razor scowled. ''Yeah, well, she ain't helpin' matters none.''

''But you could,'' Alison said, in her best Pollyanna voice. Ross was surprised that the men hadn't hooted her down yet. ''If you'd just sing something...''

Razor looked stunned that she would even ask such a thing. ''You mean like a kids' song?''

Alison smiled. ''No, like a real song.'' She looked into the cell behind him. ''Does anybody know a song?''

Ross tugged on Alison's shirt. ''Are you nuts?'' Felicity let out a lusty wail, apparently not enjoying her proximity to Razor any more than Ross did.

''How about some Peter, Paul and Mary?'' Alison suggested.

Razor sneered at her. ''Yeah, sure. How 'bout some Led Zeppelin?''

Alison beamed as if she was a teacher and Razor her star pupil. ''That would be perfect!''

Before the shocked group, Razor flicked his long greasy hair behind his ears and began to belt ''Black Dog'' to little Felicity. Almost immediately her wails turned into hiccups of delight.

''Hey, look at that!'' one of the men standing behind Razor said. He came closer to study the baby's reaction and joined in with Razor. Before long, Felicity was being serenaded by the entire felon chorus—and a few drunks, too.

Unfortunately, although the cacophony of voices raised in rock song soothed the baby, it wasn't so pleasing to adult ears. Officer Teel burst through the door.

''All right!'' he yelled. ''Cut it out!''

Ross, still smarting from their previous encounter, frowned at him. ''Who says we can't sing?''

''*I* says,'' the officer told him.

Felicity let out one of those hesitant rumbles that she usually gave as a warning. The men had stopped singing to her and she wasn't pleased.

''What's the matter with her?'' the officer asked. ''She'd finally shut up, I thought.''

''She liked the music,'' Ross told him. ''Without the music, she'll cry.''

The cop didn't like the choice.

''No singing,'' he said finally.

Felicity wailed and continued to cry for several nerve-racking minutes. Finally Officer Teel came back and unlocked Ross's cell. ''All right, all right, you can go. Just get the caterwauling kid outta here.''

''Did you talk to Earl?'' Alison asked.

''All we could get was his sister, but she said ya'll probably wouldn't be thieves, and that Earl would probably even rent his pickup for some extra dough. Mostly, though, the sheriff just wants some peace and quiet in his jail again.''

Ross wasn't going to question his luck. If they wanted to let him go, for whatever reason, then he was all for it. He gathered up the baby and followed the policeman. Felicity babbled cutely and waved her fist in parting to her grizzled bunch of new friends. Before they had left the holding tank, he could hear the good-byes Alison exchanged with the other inmates and their murmurs.

''Cool kid.''

''Yeah—likes Led Zeppelin.''

''Cute little thing, too. Just like her mother.''

Just like her mother. Music to Ross's ears. Now if he could just get the two of them to his father in time to give Henry Templeton that very impression.

The minute they had their clothes and belongings back, Ross dragged Alison to the truck and hoisted her into the driver's seat. "*You* drive," he told her. "And whatever you do, don't speed."

He dealt with Felicity and her car seat himself, not begrudging her a gurgle, hiccup or wail. He chucked her on her dimpled chin when he was through, saying, "Good going, sweetheart. We never would have gotten out of that jail without you."

"Not alive, anyway," Alison said wryly, turning the key in the ignition. "Not the way you were baiting that Razor character. You must have a death wish or something!"

She quickly pushed the car up to the speed limit while Ross got on the phone, humming "I Shot the Sheriff" as he dialed to keep Felicity's noise level down. He called Hannah again. No answer. Everywhere he called he got no information. His father's doctor wasn't in; the hospital refused to release any information; none of his father's friends knew anything more than Ross himself.

It was so frustrating!

"Ross, you can't still think your father has gone home to—"

"Die?" he finished for her.

"Stop thinking like that," she commanded him. "He might be better."

Maybe she was right. He should stop calling. He was having no luck, and being thwarted by telephone was only making him more panicky.

But *not* calling seemed nearly as bad. The next two

hours in the cab of the truck were passed in nail-biting tension. What would he find when he arrived home?

THE TENSION IN THE TRUCK was thick enough to slice, and finally Alison could stand no more. She sent Ross a sidelong glance. She knew he didn't feel like talking, and the last time they'd had a chat in the truck, it had been a prickly sort of conversation. About his old girlfriend.

Cara, she thought, still not liking the sound of the name.

But that had been before the jail. She wasn't proud of the way she'd reacted to being in stir. But the moment Ross had produced that phone, she'd felt all her hostility toward him seep out of her like air from a leaky tire. She wouldn't have been surprised if her body had made a hissing deflating noise. And then Felicity had cried like a little trouper. Everything had worked out, just as Ross promised.

For once it seemed like they were functioning as a team, which was a lot more bearable than the animosity that had hung between them earlier.

"What's the matter, Ross?"

"Nothing."

Alison again glanced at him, hunched and defeated in the corner of the cab, and felt her heart go out to him. He was worried sick about his father. She knew how upsetting family trauma could be—even if she had no family of her own to speak of. Only a mother who blamed her for letting her fiancé dump her at the altar.

She hadn't seen her mom for a year, not since right after the wedding that didn't happen. Alison had even stayed home alone that Christmas rather than deal with the pain of having to listen to her mother's pitying sighs. It was more self-pity than anything else, really. Babs Bennett thought that a daughter's first duty to her mother was to provide one thing: a rich, socially prominent son-in-law. After the disastrous non-wedding, she made it clear that Alison had failed to deliver the goods and had humiliated the family in the bargain.

Never mind that it was *Wes* who had backed out at the last minute, not Alison. Alison was the one left to pick up the pieces, and she was helpless to convince her mother that the calamity wasn't her fault.

Helpless. That was almost how Ross looked, with his boyish lock of hair falling onto his forehead. He was probably thinking about his father, and how helpless he was to influence the outcome of his illness. Just as helpless as Alison had felt. Only this was a matter of life and death. At the time the wedding had only *seemed* a matter of life and death.

No wonder Ross had gone out of his way to pull off this scheme with the baby. He was accustomed to being a mover and shaker; this plan at least gave him something to do, something to actively throw himself into while the fates played dice over his father's health.

Although she still felt lying to a dying man was ill-advised, she suddenly felt more in sympathy with Ross. She was sorely tempted to pull the truck onto the shoulder of the road and give him a hug of encouragement. To let him know she understood.

Instead, she tried to buoy up his spirits by reminding him of the task ahead.

"Why don't you tell me what the plan is?"

He turned his gaze from the road to peer at her curiously. "Plan?"

"For when we meet your father."

"Oh." He nodded, obviously having to switch mental gears. "Well, to begin with, I think I should talk to him first, get him warmed to the idea. Given how much the man loves the idea of grandchildren, that should take about ten seconds. Then I'll present the two of you to him. You're to tell him that you're a hardheaded career woman and you don't need a husband to raise a child. You can put on that suit of yours. You can look like a real feminazi when you want to, you know."

"Thank you very much."

"I only meant..."

She laughed. "I know, I know. I don't suppose we could also tell him that I happened to have amnesia and couldn't find you for a year, could we? I'm really coming across as a lowlife in your scenario."

Ross frowned in dismay. "It's just for this once."

"Won't you feel awkward? You said your father's a real family man. I might not want to get married, but how are you going to explain your own behavior or the way you're simply willing to let your daughter float out of your life?"

Ross nodded, apparently appreciating her thoroughness. "I'll tell him I've filed for visitation rights. I've got this all planned out, Alison. You don't have to worry about a thing."

She sent him a wry glance, almost glad to have the old arrogant Ross back again. "In case you've forgotten practically everything from the past twenty-four hours, your plans have gone awry before."

"Yes, but those elements were beyond my control. This time I'll be in charge of things."

She looked over at him, taking in his now-confident posture. His broad shoulders were squared, his chin was high. The vulnerability she had glimpsed just once was gone now.

Or was it?

Her mind suddenly flashed back to the kiss of that morning, which she had been fighting to put out of her mind. She remembered being pulled into his arms in a passionate needful embrace. At least subconsciously, he had craved that moment of closeness as much as she had. Maybe Ross's arrogant assuredness, his wealthy-man I-can-buy-my-way-out-of-any-problem bravado was just a facade to hide something else.

Like that flash of helplessness she'd seen. That vulnerability.

"You might be in charge, but you can count on me to do my part, Ross," she assured him. "I still don't agree completely with your motives, but I'll be behind you all the way."

He appeared almost startled for a moment. Then he nodded. "Of course you will. It's worth twenty thousand dollars to your friends at St. Felicity's."

Frustration suffused her. Couldn't he see that she was in sympathy with him? Maybe she hadn't been initially—or even up until they'd wound up in jail together. But now she'd felt like they'd been through hell and back together, and she understood the depths of his need to make his father happy one last time.

Any man who would stand up to a thug like Razor had to be pretty desperate. And who wouldn't be, when his father's life was at stake? Their squabbles over her lying about being a nun or whether his ex-girlfriend was a bubblehead seemed rather petty in comparison.

"I just wanted you to know that I'm sure your plan will work. You don't have to worry."

"I'm not worried," he said, his overly casual manner exposing his lie. "After all, as long as we both keep our wits about us, what could possibly go wrong?"

Chapter Six

"This is it."

The Templeton ranch was set a few miles in from the nearest highway, down a long winding gravel road. Why exactly it was winding was anyone's guess, because there was no need for indirectness—the large stone ranch house could be seen in the distance through the small grove of live oak surrounding it, but other than that bit of foliage, the land leading up to the place was flat and barren, punctuated only by a rail fence and about a hundred head of cattle.

As they approached the house, the world seemed strangely silent, save for the crunching sound the pickup's tires made as it rolled over the coarse gravel. There was no wind, not even a breeze, no sound of birds twittering or cattle lowing or work being done around the place. A shiver of apprehension went down Alison's spine, and she turned to check on Felicity, who looked especially sweet in the yellow checked dress and white dress shoes with tiny lacy socks that Alison had changed her into after she and Ross had switched seats. She'd wanted Felicity to look nice for her grandfather. Who knew if she'd ever have another one?

The baby stared back at her with her huge blue eyes, but made no sound. Not even a gurgle.

Even a well-behaved baby seemed like a bad omen at this point.

"I hope everything's all right," Ross said as if sensing Alison's apprehension.

Two distinct worry lines creased his wide forehead. Remembering the precarious state of his father's health, Alison felt a sharp desire to reach over and smooth those lines, or to take his hand, which was white-knuckled on the gearshift. Instead, she clasped her hands in her lap.

"I'm sure it will be," she told him, hoping she had injected a confidence she didn't actually feel into the assertion.

The battered truck passed through an iron archway, then beneath a canopy of trees leading to the circular drive in front of the house. Up close, the sprawling mansion looked much bigger, its gray stone and unique style making it appear like a hybrid of Southfork and San Simeon. In an effort to break some of the tension in the car, Alison was about to comment on the beautiful landscaping around the house when suddenly all her attention—and Ross's—was diverted by the sight of a small dark-haired woman coming out the front door to meet them.

By her outfit—a crisp blue dress and white apron—Alison guessed the woman was Hannah, the housekeeper and Ross's old nanny. She wept openly as she approached them.

"Hannah." Ross leaped out of the truck and Alison hurriedly unbuckled her seat belt, turned and reached for Felicity. Now that the time had come for her to play her part in the bizarre charade, she felt as nervous as a singer about to debut at the Met. It didn't help that, by all appearances, the news about Ross's father couldn't be good.

The baby fussed a little, but Alison's attention was focused on the conversation outside as she climbed out of the truck.

"How is he, Hannah?"

The woman could barely speak between gulping breaths. "The doctor…just left."

Alison's gaze was riveted on Ross's expression. His face turned a waxy white color. "Oh, my God."

Hannah looked at him, shaking her head, and placed her hands on his forearms. "Ross…oh, maybe I should let him tell you."

He nodded curtly. "I'll go up right away."

To Alison's surprise, he turned to her before going into the house. "Come on," he said.

"But…" She didn't know what to say, or what to do. He wanted *her* to be in the room when he spoke to his gravely ill, perhaps mortally ill, father? "Oh, Ross, I couldn't."

"Come on," he repeated more forcefully. He took her hand and tugged her behind him. Although his grip was strong, she could feel a subtle but insistent tremor in his hand. It was that vulnerability again, and it spurred her to hold Felicity close and follow him.

Ross might not want to admit it, but he needed her just now. Although what she would accomplish by being with him eluded her. She was a lousy actress. She hadn't succeeded in convincing Ross she was a nun. How convincing would she be as Ross's ex-girlfriend?

Her legs felt rubbery and weak beneath her, and tears built in her eyes. She had never had to deal with a death before or even a serious illness. The most traumatic thing she'd ever been through was her parents' divorce, or maybe Wes's absenteeism on their wedding day. She kissed the downy hair on the baby's head and, surprisingly, drew comfort from the simple act.

Babies meant hope, didn't they?

If a grandchild meant as much to Henry Templeton as Ross said it did, then maybe seeing Felicity would bolster the man, give him something to live for. Or at least make his last hours a little brighter.

Alison shuddered. Ross was so distraught now she wondered how he would handle himself if the worst came to pass. He took no notice of the house's grand marble foyer but sped toward the staircase and headed straight for his father's second-floor bedroom. Alison followed him in a fog.

They entered the dark bedroom quietly although Ross did not stop moving until he'd reached the foot of the king-size bed. One bedside lamp was on, giving the taupe-carpeted room an amber glow.

Ross looked at his father and inhaled deeply. In that breath was a sound of despair. "Dad," he said, his tone plaintive but reverent.

His father didn't respond.

Alison felt her heart catch.

Only Henry Templeton's neck and face were visible above the quilt. If she hadn't known better, Alison would never taken this man for Ross's father. He was shorter, she could tell, and stockier—his protruding stomach brought the comforter covering it up in a solid mound. His hair was completely white, and he wore a full bushy beard and mustache. Alison winced as she noted that his skin was nearly as white as his beard. He looked like a sweet old man—who was gravely ill.

''Dad,'' Ross murmured again, moving around to the side of the bed. Pale and clammy himself, he reached out and gently put a hand on the old man's shoulder. ''Dad, it's me. Ross.'' His voice hitched in his throat. ''Your son.''

Mr. Templeton's eyelids fluttered faintly.

''Can you hear me, Dad?'' Ross asked. He looked over at Alison, his face etched with pain before he turned back to his father. ''I've brought someone for you to meet. Her name's Felicity.''

This time the man's eyelids managed to open, revealing two blue eyes exactly like Ross's, only watery and bleary from illness. ''Felicity?''

Ross swallowed, then explained quickly, ''She's my daughter, your granddaughter. I wanted you to know. I wanted you to know you actually have the grandchild you always wanted.''

Henry was speechless, but he gazed with interest at Felicity. Beckoned by Ross, Alison stepped to his side. She gently settled the baby on the bed, presenting the little girl to the proud grandfather. It suddenly struck her that Felicity's round blue eyes and the old man's were nearly identical. Looking at them side by side, she could almost believe that the two *were* granddaughter and grandfather, and the poignancy of it made her feel faint with sadness.

Ross put a steadying arm about her waist, but after a moment, she wasn't sure who was anchoring whom. ''Mr. Templeton, my name is Alison,'' she said, hearing her voice catch just as Ross's had. ''Ross and I...well, we were...''

She couldn't finish. Finally the old man looked up at her, then Ross. For the first time his eyes seemed to focus sharply. "Are you this sweet little girl's mother?"

She needn't have worried about her acting abilities. Her head nodded of its own accord. "Yes, sir," she answered, barely aware of the tear trickling down her cheek.

Henry nodded. "And you love my son?"

She felt Ross's arm freeze, and for a moment she froze, too. Then she looked at Ross, into those beautiful blue eyes. The arrogance wasn't there. The spoiled rich man wasn't there. He was just a man who loved his father.

And even in this solemn moment, he was still as handsome as the devil.

How could she tell the father that she wasn't in love with his boy?

She couldn't. Instead, she nodded. "Yes, I do. Very much."

She felt Ross's hand relax and knew she had done the right thing.

Tears spilled freely down Henry's pale cheeks, and at the same time, she could have sworn she heard Ross sniffle. Who would have known that the Templetons were such a sentimental bunch? And who would have known that she'd be part of such an emotional scene? She barely controlled herself from weeping, too.

"You should be married," Henry said, his voice raspy from sleep and emotion.

Whatever well-laid plans they'd made were forgotten. Instead, to her shock, she heard herself saying, "We intend to be."

"When?"

"Just as soon as possible," Ross said, staring at Alison with unchecked gratefulness.

"Yes, as soon as we can," Alison agreed, then babbled, "Tomorrow isn't soon enough for us. Ross and I are both hopeful there will be even more children to carry on the Templeton name and business."

To her shock she heard the sound of clapping. She and Ross looked around to find Hannah standing at the foot of the bed, an expression of rapture on her face. Gone were the tears. And when they turned back to Mr. Templeton, the old man beamed a smile at them that lit up the whole dim room.

"Hallelujah!" he cried robustly. "By gum, with any luck, I'll be there to teach the little nippers all about the business. Just like I did with you, Ross."

Ross nodded, then paled. "Dad, please..." The old man seemed to be talking off his head.

Henry coughed a little, bringing two spots of red to his pale cheeks, then turned to Ross and practically hollered, "My boy, I thought I'd never live to see the day!"

Ross reached out a hand to prevent his father from sitting up. "Dad, you shouldn't get so excited."

"Excited? Why not?" Henry Templeton cried. "Good things come in threes, don't they always say? And now here's proof. First that damn fool doctor comes in and tells me that as long as I control my blood pressure I could live to be a hundred, then you bring this sweet little baby to me—" he paused to chuck Felicity under the chin "—and now you're telling me you're finally going to get hitched, and to one of the prettiest ladies I've ever had the fortune to lay eyes on, to boot! I'd say that was cause for excitement!"

As his words sank in, Alison felt a weight lift from her heart.

"Blood pressure?" Ross repeated, his voice bright with hope.

"It was hypertension putting all that stress on his heart that made him feel like he was having a heart attack," Hannah explained. "Come to find out, all he needs is monitoring and blood-pressure medication."

Ross blinked. He was still pale, but now with relief—and shock. "But just the other day...back at the hospital...you were in such pain...and all those tubes..."

"Worst pain I ever felt. You can believe I won't be skipping my medication anytime." He practically whooped with joy. "The doctor told me I might want to slow down a little. That might be hard to do now that I've got this little missy to keep up with." He reached out with his hands and braced Felicity by her tiny shoulders. The baby responded by emitting an adorable toothless cry of delight.

Alison couldn't believe it. She continued to stand by the bed, numb. So much had happened in so little time. Someone she'd thought was on the verge of death was suddenly filled to the brim with life.

And she and Ross had told him they were going to be married.

"What an angel!" Hannah cried, unable to keep her eyes off Felicity. "How old is she?"

"Six months," Alison mumbled, feeling rather uneasy. Feeling suddenly like the impostor she truly was. Like the liar she truly was.

"Six months!" Mr. Templeton bellowed. "You two ought to be ashamed of yourselves, keeping her hidden away all this time! You should have been married a year and a half ago, not tomorrow!"

All the blood drained out of Alison's face. *Tomorrow?*

"Tomorr..." Ross's voice faltered. "Oh, but—"

"You said you wanted to get married ASAP, didn't you?" Templeton nodded at his housekeeper. "Hannah, pick up that darn phone and get me Pastor Wilkins on the line. We're gonna have us a weddin'!"

Ross jumped. "Dad, no!"

Alison was glad someone had the presence of mind to stop him. She was still in such shock she needed someone to throw a blanket over her.

When his father looked up at him in dismay and Hannah halted her dialing to stare at him, Ross lowered his voice and explained haltingly, "I mean, gosh, Dad...Alison and I..." He glanced at her for help, looking more like a little boy lost than a business executive. "We wanted something...something quiet."

"Yes, a small wedding," Alison piped up finally, her heart beating like mad. What on earth were they going to do?

Wing it, was the only answer that came to her.

"Something private," she finished.

"Yeah, private," Ross echoed. "We were thinking of going somewhere by ourselves...like Las Vegas."

His father's mouth twisted in disgust. "Las Vegas!" he said sourly. "What would you want to do that for when you can have the darn thing right here, among all your friends and family and the same preacher who's been telling you to get married for almost fifteen years now? Heaven knows you waited long enough, son. I intend to see this is done up right!"

The old man gave his newfound granddaughter a playful little shake, and the two of them let out cackles of delight as Hannah resumed dialing the telephone.

"TOMORROW ISN'T SOON enough for us?" Ross tossed his hands in the air, then raked his fingers through his hair. "Did you have to put ideas into his head?"

"Me?" Alison paced fretfully in front of the huge leather sofa that Ross had collapsed into minutes before.

"Yes, you. You were the one who told him we were going to be married!"

"I was just following your lead."

He grumbled. "Yeah, well, you didn't have to do such a good job of it, did you?"

There was no sense trying to place blame now. "Ross, what are we going to do?"

He rubbed his temple. "I'm not sure," he said. "I didn't expect things to come out like this. I'm still in shock. One day he was fine, the next day he was dying… I guess I panicked."

"Oh, Ross, I'm so glad he's okay." She smiled, in spite of their little problem. Which seemed to be escalating quickly into a very big problem.

"So am I," Ross said. "My God, I'm ecstatic! It's just that, before I went up to his room and actually saw him lying there, I didn't know I would get so…so…"

"Carried away?" she finished for him.

He shook his head as if still stunned. "I don't know what came over me. I just saw him there, looking so lovingly at that baby, and then when you said we were going to get married and he looked so happy, just like I'd hoped he would, I couldn't help echoing your terrible words."

Terrible words? Alison couldn't help stinging a little at the description. She didn't want to marry Ross any more than he wanted to marry her, but he didn't have to get ugly about it. All the insecurity she'd felt when Wes had left her standing in a church vestry in a long white dress washed over her.

What was it about weddings and her that just didn't seem to mix?

She tried to focus on Ross's father and how they were going to talk him into canceling all the plans he was already busy making. "I can see why you love him so, Ross. He's so cute. You never told me he looked like Santa Claus."

Ross laughed. "I never thought about it." He smiled wryly. "I can't believe I lost control like that. Of course, I have an excuse. He's my father. Why you weren't able to keep your head is another matter entirely."

"For heaven's sake!" she said defensively. "What was I supposed to do? It was like I'd stepped into a 'Waltons' episode."

It was easier to joke now, but she couldn't forget how horrible it had been watching Ross looking at his father at death's door. She would have said she was a space alien if it would have brought the man some happiness. "It's my fault, I admit it. But pointing fingers is...pointless. We've got to try to straighten out this mix-up."

"Oh, sure, that should be a snap," Ross said.

"We have to. Your father's upstairs playing with a little girl he thinks is his grandchild and calling up everyone he knows to invite them to our wedding. Meanwhile, Hannah's in the kitchen planning a Sunday barbecue for the whole county in honor of our nuptials. If we're going to stop the wedding, we've got to do it soon—immediately."

"All right," Ross said, sitting up straight. "We'll go up right now and tell him we lied."

Alison froze. *Right now?* Put so bluntly, honesty sounded very unappealing. "How can we do that?"

"Simple. We go into his room, pry the phone out of his hand and confess the whole thing. Or at least the fact that we won't be getting married."

"But then..." Then Henry would know she'd lied about loving Ross. That she'd lied about everything. She shook her head. "I wouldn't be able to face him."

"Okay," he said. "Here's plan B. We can lie again."

"And tell him what?"

"We can make up some reason why you absolutely can't get married tomorrow."

"What reason could there be?"

"Well..." Ross thought for a moment, then snapped his fingers. "I know! We could tell him you're already married."

"What!"

"Dad might be desperate to see me married off, but I doubt he'd approve of bigamy."

"Ross, no—that's so underhanded."

He shot her a disbelieving grin. "You're afraid of telling him the truth, but you're determined not to tell any new lies, which means we'll just have to continue with the old one. There's no pleasing you."

"Don't laugh—this is serious." She collapsed into a wing chair, feeling for a moment as if she might cry. How in the world could she worm her way out of this? But then, how could she *not* worm her way out of this? She couldn't get married tomorrow—absolutely not.

She didn't have anything to wear, even.

Fleetingly she pictured herself walking down the elaborate Templeton staircase in the purple negligee Sister Joan had packed for her, a bouquet of lilies cradled in her arms. In spite of just having admonished Ross to be serious, she giggled.

"What?" Ross asked, peering at her curiously.

She waved a hand. "It's nothing."

"If you've got an idea, I need to hear it. No matter how ridiculous."

Alison smiled. "I was just wondering what my assistant Dee would think if I showed up in Dallas on Monday morning actually married."

"She'd probably think you'd given mixing business with pleasure a whole new slant."

Alison laughed, bending her knees and curling up in the chair. It felt so good to laugh, to release some of the tension that had been welling up in her.

Then she realized with dismay that she couldn't *stop* laughing. Ross watched her for a moment, then burst out laughing, too. Alison felt tears that she had tried to keep bottled up inside actually spill down her cheeks, which only made her more hysterical. Ross matched her chuckle for chuckle until they both felt completely worn-out.

Just yesterday she had run away from a convent. Now she was a hysterical bride-to-be. How on earth had she gotten herself into such a predicament?

Finally, as her breathing began to steady and Ross's laughter also died down, she heard a catch in his throat. "You know, that's not a bad idea," he said.

She couldn't imagine what he was talking about. "What?"

"You and me. Getting married."

She sent him a dubious glance. "You're kidding, right?"

"No—in fact, I should have thought of this right away. Why not?"

"Why not get married?" she repeated in disbelief. Surely he was joking. But no, he straightened and stared at her in dead earnest. "Ross, do I actually have to explain this to you?"

He popped off the couch to wear out the same five feet of carpet she'd been pacing minutes before. "Just because we get married doesn't mean we have to *stay married.*"

She shook her head emphatically. "Not on your life," she said, warning him off this line of thinking.

"But wouldn't it solve all our problems? We get married, except we're the only ones who know we're really *not* married."

"But we *would* be married," she argued.

"Then we'll get divorced."

He said it so matter-of-factly, so nonchalantly, as if divorce were the easiest thing in the world. She'd been through one divorce, her parents', and she couldn't imagine it ever being easy. "Divorce takes months, Ross! We'd be bogged down in legal entanglements for a long time."

"Well, what difference would that make?"

Alison thought for a moment before coming up with an answer—one that made her strangely uncomfortable. "What if while we were getting our divorce you fell madly in love with someone else and wanted to marry her right away?"

She took comfort in the speed with which he dismissed her scenario. "No way. Let's face it, I'm married to my work. I never intend to get married—except maybe to you of course. But that's different.''

She blinked. It was bizarre having a man talking so offhandedly about marrying her. As if it was no big deal.

''What about you?''

She stared at him. ''Me?''

''You don't have some man on the back burner, do you?'' The intense curiosity in his gaze brought heat to her cheeks.

''No, there's no one. I'm like you. I love my work.'' Not to mention, she'd been hiding in her apartment for a year, licking her romantic wounds.

''That's perfect, then.''

''Ross, no.''

He raked his hands through his hair, thinking. ''How about this? We tell them we're going to Mexico on our honeymoon. Instead, we go to Mexico and get a quickie divorce. Come next Christmas, I'll tell Dad we're separated.''

She bit her lip to keep herself calm. ''And how will you explain his granddaughter's mysterious disappearance from your life?''

His brows came together in a ridge of worry. ''That's something I'm going to have to explain whether we get married or not.''

''Can't you see this just won't work?'' she asked him plaintively. ''You're going to have to make a full confession. And soon. At least about the marriage part.''

Clearly Ross still found this idea unappetizing. ''Just give me time. I'm sure I can think of something if I put my mind to it.''

She sighed. She couldn't believe that the man who

had seemed so self-assured and businesslike when he'd stomped into her office wanting to rent a baby had suddenly, at the prospect of disappointing Daddy, turned into Mr. Mush-for-Brains. "They're inviting a hundred guests for tomorrow, Ross. The longer we put off telling the truth, the worse trouble we'll be in."

"I know you're right," he said. "I just need to think, to work this one out."

He didn't need to explain further. What he was hoping for was another *plan.*

"You do what you think is best, Ross. I'm only a paid participant in this scenario, after all."

He looked at her almost as if she'd wounded him. "You're more than that."

"What else am I, then?" she asked, hating herself for waiting breathlessly for his answer. She remembered the way his arm had relaxed around her when she'd told his father she loved him. Did he remember?

She didn't love him of course. But over the past day she'd grown close to him. After all, he was the only man she'd ever shared a cheap roadside motel room with. The only man she'd ever been to jail with...

"You're..." He started to say something, then seemed to think better of it. "You're in charge of Felicity, for one thing."

"I see." She shook her head, clearing it of the crazy feeling of disappointment. "Then I guess I'll go check on my charge."

He nodded. "I'll think of something, Alison, don't you worry. I'm going to talk to Dad before lunch."

"Fine," she said, heading toward the door. And while Einstein was thinking, she might just take it on herself to find a way to tell Mr. Templeton the reason she would not be joining his family. Just in case Ross's attempt at truth-telling didn't work out so well.

As she opened the door to the hallway, she heard another door close quickly. As if someone had been in the hall listening to them and didn't want to be caught.

Alison hesitated for a moment, then dismissed the suspicion as paranoia and started up the stairs.

"I'VE NEVER SEEN such a happy baby," Henry said, bouncing Felicity on his knee. He spread his face into a goofy grin, making Ross wonder what it was about babies that could turn grown men into Jell-O.

Felicity let out a squeal and shook her little fists with glee. Ross was amazed. Looking at her now, anyone would have thought she really was a little angel. And in fact, there hadn't been so much as a fuss or gurgle out of her since they'd presented her to Henry. The two of them belonged on a greeting card.

Guilt seeped into the back of his mind. This was exactly what he'd wanted—his father was ecstatic. He'd paid a bunch of nuns twenty thousand dollars to achieve this effect. So why didn't he feel better about it?

"Uh, Dad..."

Henry looked up. "Something worrying you, Ross?"

He tried to gather his nerve. There was no way he could tell his father the *whole* truth. Felicity had already wormed her way into Henry's heart. But he couldn't make Alison go through with a wedding just because he was too cowardly to own up to his falsehood.

There had to be a way to put off the wedding for a

little while. Once he and Alison had left the ranch, it would be much easier to tell his father that the relationship had broken up. A simple phone call would do, and save them all a big scene.

Of course, it would also make him feel like a heel.

"I was just thinking about the state of your health," Ross said. "You were so ill... I'm afraid having a wedding here would be too much too soon."

"Nonsense!" His father shook his head adamantly. "Best thing for me."

"Maybe you should talk it over with your doctor," Ross said, sensing doom.

"Doctors, phooey! I've had enough of them, thank you." He nudged Felicity nose to nose. "Haven't I, sweetie? Yes, I have!" he said, his voice several octaves higher than normal.

How could you reason with a man who was Eskimo-kissing a six-month-old?

Time for another tactic.

"The truth is, Dad," Ross began, then looked over and noticed that Henry was completely absorbed in making crinkly-nose faces at Felicity. "Dad?"

Henry glanced up at him in surprise, as if he'd forgotten Ross was even there. "Yes, son?"

Ross took a breath. "The thing is, Alison's a little shy."

"Alison's more than that. She's wonderful!" Henry exclaimed, completely missing the thrust of Ross's comment. "Honestly, Ross, I never thought you would have the good sense to hitch your star to a woman like Alison. She doesn't strike me as your type, frankly."

"Really?" Ross's interest was piqued.

"Goodness, no!" his father said. "All those things you went out with...especially what's-her-name..."

"Cara," Ross supplied.

Henry grimaced in distaste and repeated the name as though it were medicine. "Cara. That girl had no heart to her. Just a pretty face she was always checking in any reflective surface she could find."

It was true. Many was the time Ross had taken Cara out to dinner and caught her staring lovingly into her butter knife. Of course, she *was* beautiful. But then, so was Alison. And though Alison could be prickly and self-righteous and had even lied to him about being a nun most of the time he'd known her, he felt more comfortable with her after two days than he had with Cara after two years. Maybe the difference was that Alison understood her own foibles as well as she did those of other people. She had a dry sense of humor about life and wasn't afraid to turn the humor on herself sometimes.

And his father was right. She had a heart. He wouldn't have thought it when he first met her, but that was before he'd seen the look on her face when they'd gone up to see his dad. She'd looked as worried as he felt. When they'd presented Felicity to Henry, she'd had tears in her eyes. And when it had come time to lie, she had done so wholeheartedly. She'd even fibbed beyond the call of duty and said that she was in love with him, for his father's sake.

Ross was suddenly curious. The lie *had* been for his father's sake, hadn't it? It *was* a fib, wasn't it?

Of course it was!

His father reached over and grabbed his knee, squeezing it. "I'm proud of you, Ross—and happy you've found a woman to share your life with."

Ross shifted uncomfortably. "It's not that easy."

"Apparently!" Henry cried, nodding toward Felicity. "But now that you've finally convinced Alison that you love her and want to marry her, I'm sure things will work out for you. Your mother and I had some rocky moments, too, but they came after we were married, not before."

"Well, the thing is, we're still a little rockier than we may appear..."

His father was still too busy strolling down memory lane to listen to Ross's warning. "You wouldn't believe the fights Anita and I had, Ross—and over the silliest things! But would I have traded a moment? No, indeed! Neither would your mother. And right now, if she's looking down from heaven, you can be sure there's a great big smile on her face. How she would have loved to see your wedding day, son!"

This was too much. Ross stood and raked a hand through his hair. "Dad, I've got to tell you something. You've got to listen."

Ross drew up to his full height and took a calming breath. His father stared up at him, blinking in surprise. "Of course I'm listening, Ross," his father said. "What is it you want to tell me?"

Ross couldn't find the words. Why was this so difficult? In business he'd faced much more painful truths. He'd had to tell investors that they had lost hundreds of thousands of dollars. He'd had to announce layoffs to employees who would have trouble finding new jobs. But never in his life had he been as tongue-tied as now, faced with the prospect of telling his father he wasn't going to be getting married.

Even Felicity, her blue eyes huge and luminous, seemed absorbed in what Ross might have to say. Her rosebud lips were parted, and when he hesitated, she thrust her arms out at him and kicked her legs with impatience. A stream of babble issued from her mouth.

"Weh-meh-weh-dah-dah."

Henry gasped.

Ross narrowed his eyes at her. "What?"

"Didn't you hear her?" Henry asked. "She said Da-da!"

Ross almost asked what for, then he remembered. *He* was Da-da. Something, maybe some instinct that had lain dormant in him forever, tugged at his heart, and he stepped forward, picking up Felicity and lifting her high above his head. "Did you say Da-da?" he sing-songed inanely, just as Henry had been doing moments before.

"Of course she did!" Henry cried. "I heard her."

"That's right," Ross cooed, jiggling Felicity until she squealed with delight. "I'm your da-da."

Henry laughed, stood up and grabbed one of Felicity's tiny booties. "She's just as happy as I am that she and her mommy are about to join our family, aren't you, sugar?" Felicity's gurgle of an answer seemed to satisfy him, and he turned his attention back to Ross. "Now what was it you wanted to tell me, son?"

Chapter Seven

"Won't any of your family come for the ceremony, Alison?"

Alison's cheesecake-laden dessert fork froze halfway on its journey to her mouth. She looked from her plate to the expectant eyes staring at her. So far she had floated through dinner, smiling and mumbling appropriate responses when necessary, trying to pretend all this incessant wedding talk really had nothing to do with her. But here was a thorny question she would simply have to explain.

"It's all happening so suddenly," she said. "And my parents...well, they divorced when I was in junior high..."

She still had a glimmer of hope that Ross would find a way to tell his father the truth. Yet all day when she'd pressed him on the issue, he'd been evasive, muttering about figuring out a new plan and Felicity calling him Da-da. And the few times she had gathered the courage to look at him during dinner, trying to show him how uncomfortable the whole situation was becoming, he darted his eyes away.

Hannah and Henry were so overcome by marriage fever that they didn't appear to notice that neither the potential bride nor groom shared their enthusiasm for tomorrow's ceremony.

"Oh, what a shame!" Hannah said. She turned to Alison, her eyes eagle-sharp in their scrutiny. "No one to give you away?"

Suddenly an idea hatched in Alison's head. If she simply said that her father would never forgive her if she didn't invite him, then perhaps she could stall the wedding for a few days. Naturally she wouldn't actually try to locate her father—whom she hadn't seen for years—just pretend she was trying to. "My father would feel terrible if he wasn't here to give me away. But I'm not sure where I can find him on such short notice."

"You're right!" Ross said, understanding dawning in his eyes. "No telling where he'll be. It could take us days to find him."

Henry frowned. "Well, that's too bad. But don't you worry, Alison. We'll videotape the whole thing for him. I've got a beaut of a camera."

"Dad," Ross said, "don't you think we should *wait* to have the ceremony when Alison's father can be present?"

Henry thought for a moment, then shrugged. "Oh, I don't see the necessity for that. I'd be glad to march down the aisle with Alison."

"But..."

But their arguments hardly mattered. Hannah and Henry left the subject of Alison's relatives far behind and launched into a heated discussion of flowers. As Alison sat smiling and nodding, it was decided that she should carry gardenias from one of the flower gardens in back, and that the house would be decorated with camellias, asters, snapdragons and an assortment of other posies. Hannah would oversee the collection of the flowers in the morning.

Perversely Alison actually fancied the idea of carrying gardenias. From the deepest recesses of her mind came memories of that day a year ago, the one on which she was supposed to become Mrs. Wesley Westerbrook. She'd had a rose bouquet—one that never got carried down the aisle or tossed to bridesmaids.

She didn't know what happened to it after she left the church, distraught. Of course, she herself hadn't fared so well after that day. She'd been all keyed up, ready to begin married life. But instead, she'd spent a year wallowing in wedding-disaster limbo. The thought of walking down the aisle with a bouquet of gardenias and actually getting married seemed almost cathartic. Like post-traumatic-stress victims who reenact their moment of truth, trying to visualize a different outcome so they can recover and get on with their lives.

"The marriage license!"

Alison jerked up, startled.

The others ceased their chatter to stare inquisitively at Ross, whose eyes sparkled with something between pride and relief.

"What are you yelling about?" Henry asked his son.

In a split second Alison understood Ross's meaning perfectly. Of course—they didn't have a marriage license. No marriage license, no wedding!

Ross made a point of shooting Alison a sympathetic look. "Honey, I'm so sorry! Today has been such a whirl I totally forgot about the license."

"Oh, darn," Alison said, almost feeling the disappointment she was feigning. She'd been a little too carried away by the gardenia scenario. She forced an expression of bitter regret. "How could we be so thoughtless!"

"I feel just terrible about it." Ross turned to his father with a heavy sigh. "It will be a pain to call all those guests and tell them not to come, but I suppose it has to be done."

"Thank heavens we didn't cull all those flowers yet," said Hannah, apparently more concerned about the well-being of her garden than the wedding of Ross and Alison.

"Yes, thank heavens!" Alison chimed in. Despite her wedding-day fantasies, relief flooded through her.

"Nonsense!" Henry cried.

Hannah looked up hopefully, and Ross and Alison locked gazes of dread across the table.

"Nonsense?" Ross echoed.

A license was minor stuff to Henry. "Why, if a man can't oil the wheels of bureaucracy when it's really important, what's the durn use of being a multimillionaire?"

"You mean you think you can arrange to get us a license on a Saturday night?" Ross asked doubtfully.

"Saturday night, my foot!" his father exclaimed. "I'll get 'em for you tomorrow morning—on a Sunday! Don't you youngsters worry about a thing. I've got it all under control."

No doubt he did, a fact that made Alison very nervous. Both she and Ross had tried their best to think of reasons to delay their wedding, but so far their efforts had fallen on deaf ears. She considered bringing up her lack of a wedding dress as an excuse—but if Henry Templeton could finagle a marriage license, it was a cinch that he could scrounge up a wedding gown.

It looked as if the wedding was actually going to occur.

But how could she go through with it?

When Henry stretched and stood up from the table, it seemed her last best hope for escaping imminent matrimony was slipping away.

She turned to Felicity, who was covered in food from Alison's less-than-successful attempts to get her to eat some strained peas. Not only was the baby a mess, but every square inch around her for a circumference of about two feet seemed to contain a dollop of green.

"Poor lamb!" Hannah declared, looking at Felicity. "She'll need a bath. Would you mind terribly if I tended to her? It's been so long since I've had a chance to be around a baby."

Alison readily agreed, handing a squirming, no doubt soon-to-explode Felicity over to the older woman. "I'll be up to check on your progress in a few minutes, in case you need rescue."

Hannah shook her head, then shot a meaningful glance Ross's way. "I've handled more ornery bundles than this one in my day."

When they were gone, Alison found herself alone in the dining room. Ross had disappeared into the parlor in which they had sat just that afternoon, and his father had strolled out to the veranda off the side of the house. Had Ross given up all hope of trying to halt the wedding, or was he just regrouping, attempting to think of more excuses?

Maybe that was the problem. Excuses were getting them nowhere. It was time for some truth.

Alison took a deep breath and stood. Maybe she would have more luck with the direct approach. She set her sights on the veranda and Henry.

He was already seated on a chaise longue when she got there. "You should be upstairs resting," she admonished him, taking a seat on a chair beside him.

"Nonsense," he grumbled, then laughed. "The way you're bossing me around, you must be feeling like one of the family already."

She swallowed. "That's what I meant to talk to you about, sir."

"Please, Alison, call me Henry."

"All right...Henry," she said uneasily, giving in to his wish. She cleared her throat before going on. "Like I said, there was something I wanted to talk to you about."

He winked knowingly. "If it's about that dear little baby, don't you give it another thought. I might look like an old-fashioned coot to you, but believe me, I know how these things can happen. What's important is that you and Ross are getting married after all, and settling down with your family."

A flush heated her cheeks. "That's not exactly—"

"You know," he said, leaning back and squinting philosophically, "I guess all parents look forward to the day their child finds that special someone and settles down. Means you can stop worrying so much about them. Oh, I know I've always given Ross the business about wanting grandchildren, but what I really wanted was to know he was settled, happy. I know I'll rest easier after tomorrow."

He sent her a broad smile, and Alison swallowed past the lump in her throat. He wasn't making her task any easier. "Yes, I can see how you might. But you know—"

"And I must say, I can't imagine Ross picking a better woman than you, Alison," he said before she could finish.

Now she knew where Ross's infuriating habit of interrupting her came from. Feeling more and more like a deceptive worm the longer Henry went on, she opened her mouth to protest, but once again he stopped her.

"Now, now, don't be modest. A bride shouldn't be, you know."

She wanted to tell him to quit saying these things, that she wasn't really a bride, she was an impostor. There was no way she could go through with a fake marriage tomorrow—the idea was ludicrous. All she had to do was open her mouth and tell him so.

Unfortunately his mouth was quicker on the draw. "I suppose you'll think me a sentimental old fool for saying this, but when you and Ross went downstairs this afternoon, leaving me with my little granddaughter, I wept. With joy," he clarified, his blue eyes practically tearing up again as he spoke. "I know Ross sets a lot of store by the Templeton business—more than I ever did, even—but I never thought I'd see him treasure a single person so much. That changed when I noticed the way he looked at you."

The shock of Henry's words nearly sent her rocketing out of her chair; yet at the same time no amount of money would have convinced her to leave, instead of asking in a high-pitched croak of disbelief, "At *me?*"

"Of course you!" he answered, chuckling. "Who else?"

The revelation caught her off guard. Of course Henry had to be mistaken—Ross had been too anxious about his father's health to spare her much more than a glance.

And yet...*had* he looked at her when she wasn't paying attention? They had been around each other such a short period of time she really hadn't had the opportunity to wonder what Ross thought of her. She knew he found her attractive—he'd flirted with her even when she was a nun. She assumed his feelings were simple lust...but maybe Henry saw more than she had been able to.

Or maybe he really was just a sentimental old fool, reading nonexistent meanings into situations....

Or maybe Ross was growing as attached to her as she had become, grudgingly, to him. The thought gave her pause.

And then she dismissed it.

Nonsense! A simple lustful glance spied by his father didn't change the fact that they were embroiled in a situation from which they simply had to extricate themselves before it was too late. She willed the beating of her heart to slow—an activity that stole precious seconds from her game plan. Henry surprised her this time by reaching over and covering her hand with his.

"I'm sorry about your family, Alison. That your father and mother won't be here tomorrow." He slanted a curious gaze at Alison. "Is your mother's name Felicity, too?"

Alison shook her head. "No, her name is Barbara. Babs. She lives in Dallas, but we've been estranged since...well, for a while." Naturally, she couldn't explain to Henry that Babs thought Alison was defective for not marrying the man of her mother's dreams.

"Then Felicity was named after...?"

Alison couldn't think of any answer but the truth. "A convent."

Henry drew back. "You don't say!"

"Yes, I know some nuns from St. Felicity's in Dallas, and I even spent some time there once..." She tried to make it sound as if "once" was years ago, instead of just last week, when she'd attempted to Wes-proof herself. Strange. All that *did* seem very far away now.

"Ah, I see," Henry whispered, drawing his own conclusions. He probably thought she'd stayed there to have the baby, because his grip on her hand tightened. "I don't want you to think that little baby is the only kin you'll have on hand tomorrow, my dear. I want you to consider the whole Templeton tribe as your family. I assure you, that's how we already think of you."

He squeezed her hand again, and as he did so, Alison felt as if a steel band were squeezing around her heart. Within hours it seemed as if she had become closer to this sweet old gentleman than she was to her own parents. It was easy to understand now why Ross would be willing to resort to subterfuge to fulfill his father's dearest wish. Henry, with his kindness, good humor and burly Santa-like features, also made her want to be more generous than she had heretofore thought possible.

He dearly wanted this wedding to take place. Suddenly, with her hand still enveloped in his large comforting paw, she felt tears spring to her eyes. She was remembering how happy her mother had been as they'd prepared for her wedding.

Babs had thought that Wes hung the moon, and that

marrying him was going to be the best thing that ever happened to Alison. Maybe the best thing that ever happened to herself, too. Babs had lavished such attention to detail on Alison's upcoming ceremony that even now Alison suspected it would have been a beautiful event—even if she had been marrying the wrong man.

She and her mother had not been close since that time. In fact, they had been avoiding each other like the plague. But now Alison couldn't help feeling a little wistful. Maybe they were sentimental and sometimes silly affairs, but weddings meant something, especially to parents.

Tomorrow's wedding certainly meant something to the parent sitting next to her. Why should she go out of her way to deprive Henry of the happiness of seeing his son married?

Even if it wasn't a real marriage.

''Why, you're trembling,'' Henry said softly, his blue eyes gently probing hers. ''Was there something else you wanted to tell me, Alison?''

She looked at Henry, speechless for a moment, wondering how she could possibly have thought she could tell him what she had originally meant to say. She certainly couldn't now.

She blinked, shaking her head innocently. ''No.'' He was still watching her curiously. ''Unless...''

''Unless what?'' he asked when she didn't finish.

She smiled, unable to resist his wide-eyed eagerness to help her, the almost complete stranger whose only bond to him was that she was about to marry his only son. A lot of fathers would have reacted completely differently to a son bringing home a strange woman and her child.

In an instant she knew she was making the right decision.

"I was just..." She hesitated, unable to stop a modest bridelike blush from creeping into her cheeks. "I was just wondering if you meant it when you offered to give me away."

A smile that could have lit up West Texas was beamed back at her. "My dear, I'd be delighted!"

FINALLY! ROSS HAD BEEN searching everywhere for his father and/or Alison, and here they were, hiding in a barely lit corner of the side porch.

Resolve made him look a little grimly on the intimate setup. He had failed Alison at dinner and then afterward hadn't been able to think of anything else that would convince his father that the wedding couldn't take place. Which left the awful truth. Yet what choice did he have? Alison's pretending to be the mother of his child was one thing, but actually going through with a marriage ceremony was quite another. He couldn't let her do it.

He snapped the sliding doors closed behind him loudly enough that the two figures on the veranda turned to stare at him.

"Am I interrupting something?" he asked.

He was taken aback by the flushed startled look on Alison's face. What had the two of them been talking about?

His father stood. "Not interrupting a thing—in fact, I was expecting you earlier. If this was my gal, you wouldn't see me leaving her alone on a moonlit night."

If she was my gal, I wouldn't, either.

Now where had that crazy thought come from?

Strange thing was, now that it occurred to him, he knew it was the truth. Seeing Alison sitting there, obviously in distress about something, made his heart feel suddenly too big for his chest. If she was his girl, he would have gone over right that moment, pulled her into his arms and kissed all her worries away.

But sensing that *he* was her main worry, he realized how much of a fantasy that image was. The best thing he could do for Alison right now was to clear up the wedding charade.

''Dad, I need to tell you something,'' he said, feeling a little like the recalcitrant Beaver Cleaver.

Alison's eyes widened in alarm. ''Oh, Ross, can't it wait until morning?''

'''Course it can,'' his father said jovially. ''I'm going to leave you two lovebirds alone now.''

''That's what I want to talk to you about, sir,'' Ross said, screwing up his courage. ''It's about me and Alison.''

Faster than the blink of an eye, Alison was out of her chair and at his side, hanging on his arm, looking up at him pleadingly. ''Your father and I have already discussed this, Ross. It's just as you said—he doesn't care one whit about our not being married when Felicity was born.''

''Well, now, I wouldn't go that far,'' Henry said, puffing out his chest philosophically. ''But as long as you two are putting things to rights...well, I don't see what harm's been done.''

''There, you see?'' Alison said, her gaze meaningful.

What was the matter with her? Didn't she understand that he was finally going to tell his father the truth, just like she'd wanted all along?

Apparently she did. And she didn't want him to tell the truth.

Had his father somehow convinced Alison to go through with the wedding? If so, Ross couldn't let her do it. He felt guilty for even suggesting it to begin with. He took a deep breath, preparing to plunge right in. "Dad, there's something you should know. Alison and I aren't—"

"Aren't going to be living near the ranch," Alison jumped in.

Ross's mouth was still hanging open, preparing to say "getting married tomorrow" when Alison's words sank in. He turned to her in surprise.

She stared innocently back at him. "You're not angry I told him, are you?"

They both looked at Henry, who wore a look of resigned disappointment on his face. "I guess I should have expected it."

"It's just that my business is in Dallas," Alison explained coolly. "I hope you'll understand, Henry."

Even if he still wanted to clear things up—which he did—Ross didn't know where to begin now. Alison and his father were a step ahead of him, and his footing was so unsure that he feared every time he opened his mouth he was stepping into a verbal minefield. He didn't want to bungle the situation any more than he already had.

At least not until he had talked to Alison alone and could figure out where they stood.

Henry shook his head. "When Ross's mother and I got married, we lived the first two years in the back of her parents' house. And you know what?"

"What?" Alison said.

"I was never so miserable in my life!" He let out

a snort. "I felt self-conscious every minute of my time around her folks. They were so resentful that I had stolen their daughter away—and I hadn't even managed to be able to steal her away to another neighborhood. Yes sirree, I can certainly sympathize with you two wanting some space of your own."

Alison let out a sigh of relief—as if she had actually been worried about explaining to his father where they were going to live. Ross was amazed at what a good actress she was.

"Just so I get to see my grandbaby every once in a blue moon, that's all I ask."

"Of course," Alison readily agreed, squeezing Ross's arm. "We wouldn't have it any other way."

Ross shook his head. This from the woman who had been telling *him* how shameless and scheming he was mere days before!

The squeeze on his arm turned into a painful pinch. Alison looked up at him through impatient eyes and cued, "Would we, Ross?"

"N-no," he stammered.

"Naturally," Henry continued, seeing nothing amiss in the soon-to-be newlyweds' behavior, "I'll want to start a college fund."

Ross shifted impatiently. "Dad, I'm sure we'll be able to scrape up enough money to send our child to college."

His father's eyes narrowed. "I've never seen you turn your nose up at money before."

Alison laughed, alleviating some of the tension between the two men. "Ross, before you start turning down money on our daughter's behalf, I think we should consult Felicity on the issue."

Alison looped her arm around his waist and gave him a forceful tug in the direction of the double doors.

Henry laughed. "I'm glad one of the girl's parents has her head screwed on right!"

"In fact," Alison continued with a nod of her head for Ross, "we can go discuss the matter with her now. It's time to put her to bed."

"Don't let me keep you," Henry said. "I'm about ready to hit the hay myself."

They said good-night to Henry on the veranda and were halfway up the stairs arm in arm before Ross thought it safe to ask in a whisper, "What the heck is going on?"

"We're getting married tomorrow, that's what," Alison said. There was a finality in her tone that told him right away that arguing the issue was pointless.

"But why?" he asked. "I thought—"

Alison put a finger to her lips as they stood outside the spare room allotted to her, where Felicity's crib had been set up. Once they looked in and saw the baby sleeping peacefully, she whispered, "Because you were right. I couldn't tell him the truth. This wedding means too much to him."

"I can't let you go through with it, Alison. I realize now *you* were right. The lies have to stop."

"They will...soon," she said. "After we're married."

He looked down into her brown eyes, took in the definite gleam in them, along with the hint of color in her cheeks. *After they were married?* The phrase seemed so improbable, so ridiculous...so tempting.

Alison's brows furrowed in worry. "Ross?"

It took him a moment to snap out of whatever spell those brown eyes had him under. Of course, after they were married, they would start about the business of getting a divorce. "I don't know what to say," he said in a low throaty voice. "You shouldn't—"

Quickly, with the sweetest smile he'd ever seen playing across her full mouth, she lifted a finger to his lips to silence his protest. "Just say thanks," she murmured.

Her simple touch made every atom in his body come alive with desire. Her voice made him want her more than he had ever wanted any woman. Was it kismet, he wondered, or simply the fact that this extremely beautiful woman was saving his bacon?

Right now he didn't care. All he knew was that he couldn't resist bending down and placing a kiss on those lovely lips. She gave a start at the soft pressure of his lips on hers, then melted into him, draping her arms about his neck seductively.

This would mark the first time a woman had seduced him in his parents' house; but for all he knew at the moment, his surroundings could have been a suite at the Ritz or a desert harem: the only thing on his mind was Alison, and how soft her skin was, and how warm and inviting her tongue felt against his.

And how much he wanted to do more than just kiss her.

Did she feel the same? Her body was telling him yes, inviting him to explore its curves and softness. He ran a hand down her back, loving the way she arched against him in response, seeking to get closer still. Slowly the same hand moved to massage her hip, and then moved upward toward her breasts as he nipped gently at the curve of her neck.

She moaned. "Oh, Ross..."

The way she said his name almost made him lose

his mind. Almost made him forget that she *wasn't* actually his wife—and wouldn't truly be, ever. The wedding tomorrow wouldn't be real. What a fiasco it would be—and how confusing—if they set out on their fake marriage as new lovers.

With a groan he peeled himself away from her. He'd just been carried away by the moment. And by gratitude. And, okay, he'd also been carried away by some very real lust.

But he didn't want her to think he'd lost his grip on reality.

"I'll take care of everything, Alison," he assured her.

Those brown eyes looked at him dreamily through heavy lids. "Mmm..." she murmured.

"I mean it," he went on, not sure she understood him. "You can go anywhere you want."

The eyes blinked, then widened. She took a step back, her arms falling stiffly to her sides. "Go?" she repeated.

"For the divorce," he told her. "Believe me, I realize that I owe you, big time. I'll spare no expense. You can fly anywhere you want."

She crossed her arms, nodding. "You mean—?"

"Puerto Vallarta, Cancun—anywhere you want to go until the divorce goes through."

She continued to stare at him for a moment, then shook her head. "I get it. You were just sealing a bargain. And perhaps this would be the perfect moment to broach the subject of prenuptial agreements."

He frowned. What was she talking about? "No, I don't see the need for that. I trust you."

"I'm flattered." Her lips turned up in a sour smile. "Thanks. Thanks a lot," she said, taking a step into the room she shared with Felicity and shutting the door in his face.

Ross hesitated by the door, unwilling to simply walk away and let her stew. How had a kiss upset her so?

Or was it ending it that had set her off? He cocked his head, wondering. He felt like a clod, but what else could he have done? He didn't want to complicate their relationship more than it already was.

Did she?

Now *that* was an interesting question. One that would probably keep him up for hours.

He smiled. "Good night, Alison. Sleep well."

He listened for a moment.

There was no reply.

Chapter Eight

Alison was less than thrilled by Ross's largesse.

Okay, she'd been a fool to listen to Henry's talk about the way Ross looked at her. Of course he wasn't in love with her or anything like that—he'd only known her for slightly more than a day. But this was the first time a man had kissed her passionately and then made her an offer of divorce!

She tried to put it out of her head as she changed into her purple lingerie. But it was a little hard to forget about Ross, considering the fact that tomorrow was going to be her wedding day and he was, after all, her groom. She padded about the room and bathroom, getting ready for bed. Felicity awoke and beckoned Alison with chubby adorable arms. Alison inspected Felicity's impossibly tiny fingernails as she sang a lullaby-soft verse of "These Boots Are Made for Walkin'."

The change in the baby seemed amazing to her. Hard to believe Felicity was the same tot known in Dallas as the photographer's bane. She hadn't really been so cranky, after all, not once you learned the trick to dealing with her. Alison had never really felt so close to one of her clients before; yet, at the moment, with Felicity cradled into her arms, appreciating her version of Nancy Sinatra's song as no one else ever had, Alison had a hard time thinking of her as a client. She looked down at the precise moment Felicity's head nodded off to sleep on her shoulder and felt an unfamiliar stab in her heart.

Don't bond, she told herself as she settled Felicity into the fancy carved crib Henry had ordered brought down from the attic for his new grandbaby. *None of this is real.*

Except the wedding. That would be real enough.

Every time she shut her eyes as she attempted to sleep that night, Alison envisioned herself marching down the big staircase toward the Templeton parlor, which was bedecked in fragrant flowers, as Hannah had promised. But something always went wrong.

In several dreams—nightmares, really—Alison had marched down the big staircase with Henry, past all the guests, only to find *Wes* waiting for her at the opposite end of the parlor. Next to him stood her own mother, grinning happily.

The last one of those caused her to shoot up in bed, clammy and cold.

"Alison! Alison! Are you all right?"

Alison closed her eyes against the light in the room and rubbed her temples to ease the ache building there. Could it be morning already? And was the dream she had so vivid that even awake she was hearing her mother's voice?

"Alison, for Pete's sake, wake up. I've got Wes on the phone!"

The words were spoken in a whisper that was almost a hiss. It sounded just like her mother. What was more, the words seemed just like something her mother would say.

Her heart thumped in dread. *Her mother? Here?* Dear God, no!

Squinting, Alison allowed one eye to open just enough to confirm her worst fear. There, dressed in a coral suit with big black buttons and a matching hat complete with a coral plume, stood her mother, her white-knuckled hand covering the mouthpiece of the telephone's receiver.

"Thank goodness, you're awake," her mother said in her most businesslike fashion. "Now you can talk to him. Tell him you've made a horrible mistake and you're ready to go back, honey. It's not too late!"

Alison twitched her head, trying to shake the fuzziness out of it. "Mother, what are you doing here?"

"I was invited to your wedding," Babs informed her. "By that Templeton character. Your *wedding.* You can't imagine my horror. Honestly, Alison, a rancher? You've simply got to get on the phone and apologize."

Alison tilted her head. "Apologize to whom?"

Her mother looked at her as though she were as thick as a sequoia stump. "To *Wes.*" She mouthed the name more than spoke it and once more thrust the phone at her. "Go on, honey."

Alison closed her eyes again and counted to ten. *This can't be happening. Can't be.* She let out a nervous chuckle and said, "I really need some coffee. For a moment it sounded like you were telling me that you actually had *Wes* on the phone."

Her mother nodded fervently. "But I do! I've got the mute button on, but he's waiting for you, Alison."

The full horror of it finally dawning on her, Alison

leaped out of bed. "Mother, are you insane? Did you *call* him?"

"Of course."

"But why?"

"Because I can't simply stand by while my daughter marries someone she doesn't love." Her perfectly made-up face contorted into a kind of sympathetic agony. "Oh, darling, you should have told me all about your problem..." She nodded toward the crib, where Felicity stood on shaky, chubby legs, gripping the hand-carved edges with those tiny fingers, watching their goings-on with interest. "I would have understood."

"Understood what?"

"That you were hiding in shame because you were carrying Wes's child." Tears sprouted in Babs's eyes. "Oh, honey, don't you know I would have been there at the hospital with you? Don't you know that's a mother's place—to be with her daughter on that special day?"

Alison blinked, wishing she could pinch herself and discover this was really a dream, after all. "Mom, things aren't how they seem."

"I know!" her mother said excitedly, keeping her voice low and throwing an occasional furtive glance toward the door. "Your father-in-law-to-be—God forbid!—flew me in early this morning, but, honey, I checked out the commercial-plane schedules, and we can sneak you out and get you back to Dallas before noon. I'm sure of it."

Alison crossed her arms, taking a stab at patience. "And then what?" she asked. She had to hear this.

Her mother moved in conspiratorially. "Then we go see Wes. He's from such a good upstanding family—

I'm sure they would understand about little what's-its-name.'' She nodded dismissively at Felicity, causing anger to build inside Alison.

''You know how people like that think about blood ties,'' her mother went on. ''Wes's parents wouldn't want a grandchild just floating around out there out of their control. Don't you see? If you play your cards right, this might be precisely the right time to snag Wes for good.''

Alison rolled her eyes. ''Mother, you've been watching too much 'Santa Barbara.' This baby in no way belongs to Wes.''

''Then you…?'' Her mother looked as if she might cry. ''You *cheated* on Wes?''

Alison laughed in spite of herself, then turned to her mother in all seriousness. Somehow, before one or the other of them wound up on their deathbed, she fully intended to make the Wes situation perfectly clear to her mother. ''Mother, I have not cheated on Wes. I couldn't possibly have cheated on Wes. Wes dumped me, Mother. You were there! Why can't you understand that Wes wants nothing to do with me?''

Her mother's chin darted out in a pout. ''Darling, you're upset.''

''Yes, I am,'' Alison said, growing more heated with each word. ''I haven't seen you in a year, and when I do, you're still whining about Wes—as if *he* was the wronged party!''

''But I wouldn't even care, sweetheart, except that I know you must have done something to chase him away.''

It was hopeless. ''Mother, you've got to give it up. Maybe I did do something to chase him away, but

even so, that's the end of it. Wes and I are finished, and have been for a whole year now."

Her mother stood before her, biting her coral-lipsticked lip in thought. Finally she asked in a disappointed half whisper, "Then I take it you don't want to talk to Wes?"

At the end of her rope, Alison snatched the phone out of her mother's hand and pressed the mute button. Before she could second-guess her rash action, she blurted out in as chipper a voice as she could muster, "Wes? Hi, it's Alison."

She heard the familiar sound of a throat clearing on the other end of the line, but before he could get any words out, she said in a rush, "It was so nice of you to call and wish me good luck on my wedding." She knew her voice sounded like she was on over-chirp, but she didn't care. "I know you'd just love Ross Templeton if you could meet him—but I'm so in love with him I naturally expect everyone else to be, too. He's such a sweetheart, I can't tell you how relieved it makes me that you walked out on me on our wedding day. Isn't it funny how things always work out for the best? Well, thanks again for calling, Wes. Think of me the next time you're staying at a luxurious Templeton Inn. Goodbye!"

Before the man had a chance to get a word in edgewise, she slammed the phone down on its cradle. Having to face Wes, even just as a disembodied voice on the telephone, was more than she could bear. Bad enough that she now had to deal with her mother.

She looked up at Babs and forced a smile. "There. I talked to him. Happy now?"

To her surprise, her mother was smiling, too. "Did

you say Templeton *Inns?* As in, the national hotel chain?''

Alison pursed her lips. It sure didn't take much to win her mother over. ''International,'' she corrected. ''They're just now opening a posh new resort in the Swiss Alps. Ross is working on that one personally.''

A series of expressions crossed her mother's face. Disbelief. Dawning realization of the scope of the Templetons' wealth. And finally unadulterated joy.

''I can't wait to meet your new young man!'' her mother cried enthusiastically. Turning, she took another look at Felicity in her crib and beamed. ''What a beeeeeaaauuutiful little baaaaaaby!''

Felicity's face broke out in a toothless smile, as if she couldn't be more pleased to have acquired another grandparent.

''She looks just like you did, Alison,'' Babs said, tweaking Felicity's nose. Felicity babbled happily. She was hands-down adorable.

''Oh, but—''

''Just like a beautiful itty-bitty munchkin.''

It was practically the nicest compliment her mother had ever paid her. ''Really?'' Alison asked. ''*I* was a cute baby?''

''Of course!'' Now not only resigned to the wedding, but also its staunchest advocate, her mother could hardly take her eyes off her grandbaby. She clutched Felicity's tiny hands and clapped them together playfully.

Alison couldn't help laughing. She'd never seen her mother coo and squeal and make a general fool out of herself before. Babies just seemed to do that to people.

Of course she also hadn't seen her mother, period, for an entire year. As reunions went, this one was going pretty smoothly. She decided to keep her mouth shut about Felicity—about the whole screwy wedding setup. After all, the fewer people who knew the truth, the easier time they would have fooling Ross's father. There would be one less chance of a slipup.

"I think she has her father's nose," Alison said, falling easily into the lie. She put on the robe that matched her purple nightgown.

Her mother studied the baby's nose like an art enthusiast would study a sculpture by Rodin. "Hmm. Well, since I've never seen Ron, I wouldn't know."

"Ross," Alison corrected.

"Ross, of course," her mother said. "Though perhaps I would know him now by his absolutely perfect nose—if you're right and it *does* look like Felicity's."

A chuckle sounded from the doorway. "Well, maybe like Felicity's if she'd played four years of football."

Alison heard her mother draw in a breath as she turned and saw Ross. She did, too. It seemed her heart always beat a little faster when Ross was in the room.

Ross came forward, smiling that movie-star smile of his, and introduced himself. "You must be Alison's mother."

"Just call me Babs," she gushed.

He glanced questioningly at Alison as he shook her mother's hand. "Dad told me he had flown you in from Dallas as a surprise for Alison."

"I was surprised, all right," Alison said, trying to telegraph with her eyes the fact that her mother was not party to their secret.

Ross reached over and snaked an arm about Alison's waist, letting her know with a simple squeeze that he understood the situation.

"The two of you look like the perfect couple!" Babs exclaimed.

Ross grinned. "That's because we're so much in love." He dragged Alison even closer to his side. "I can't tell you how happy your daughter's made me, Mrs. Bennett."

Apparently not seeing Alison's grimace, Babs wagged her finger at Ross. "Uh-uh-uh—you promised to call me Babs."

He blushed in an aw-shucks Jimmy Stewart kind of way. "Oh, right...Babs."

She beamed.

It was all being laid on too thick for Alison's taste. Especially from a man who just the night before had been trying to reassure her about the divorce plans. She peeled herself from Ross's embrace and crossed to the baby. "If you two will excuse me, I need to see to Felicity's breakfast."

Her mother was by her side in an instant. "No, no, no—darling, this is your *day*." She lifted Felicity out of her cradle and wrinkled her nose. "Grandmommy will see to little Felicity's breakfast. Won't she, sweetie?" She bounced Felicity a few times as if actually expecting an answer.

Alison could just imagine that coral suit caked in a glaze of applesauce. "But the food's down in the kitchen. I'd better—"

Her mother would hear none of it. "*I'm* going, and that's that. Don't worry so much, Alison. I took care of you, didn't I?"

Alison laughed. "And look how I turned out," she quipped.

Babs frowned, then tossed an impatient glance at Ross. "She's always kidding."

"I don't remember starving or being dropped, if that's what you mean," Alison admitted. She just remembered being a nervous wreck by the time she was seven. But Felicity would be okay in Babs's care for an hour. Probably. "Have at it, Mother."

Babs sashayed out of the room with her precious cargo, leaving Alison and Ross alone. Alison suddenly felt self-conscious—and too aware of the flimsy nightgown set she was wearing, while Ross was fully dressed in jeans and a casual knit shirt.

She took another step back in the general direction of the dresser that contained her clothes and crossed her arms over her chest nervously. Ross looked as cool as a cucumber.

She glanced at him with a frown. "Don't you know it's bad luck to see the bride before the ceremony?"

He smiled a million-watt smile that made her insides do a flip-flop. "You don't look very bridelike."

Alison fought back a blush at the unveiled appreciation in Ross's eyes as he took in her bare legs. "You forget, I'm only a bride in the technical sense."

"Then silly wedding-day rules shouldn't apply, should they?" he asked, coming farther into the room.

"This is without question the craziest thing I've ever done in my life," she said. "And now my mother's here to witness it!"

Ross shook his head in commiseration. "I'm sorry. Bringing her here was a maverick act on Dad's part. I had nothing to do with it."

"I know, I know." Alison turned and started pulling clothes out of the dresser. "Well, if nothing else, maybe this has cured her of her obsession with Wes."

"Your ex-fiancé?"

"Yes!" Alison flopped down on the bed, laughing.

"You wouldn't believe it—she woke me up this morning with every intention of spiriting me out of your father's house and hauling me back to Dallas, to Wes, certain I was making a dreadful mistake. She'd even called him on the phone."

Ross frowned. "Did you talk to him?"

"Oh...briefly." Alison blushed a little, remembering how she'd sang Ross's praises over the phone to Wes. The poor man had probably been having a quiet Sunday morning at home, minding his own business. He also probably hadn't thought of Alison in a year. She must have sounded like a crazy woman.

Ross shifted uncomfortably. "Well, if it's any consolation, your mother seemed to like me."

"Like you?" Alison asked, gaping at him. "She loved you! And why wouldn't she? You're every mother's dream of a son-in-law. Good-looking, well mannered, rich... What more could she ask for?"

"Gee, thanks," Ross grumbled, as if she'd just insulted him. He sat on the bed in a pout.

"What's the matter?" Alison asked.

"Nothing."

"Ross..."

"Nothing," he repeated curtly.

"Then why do you look as if I'd just called you a bad name?"

He shrugged. "Maybe a man would like to be something more to the woman he's about to marry than good-looking and rich."

Alison rolled her eyes. "I was talking about what my mother thinks of you."

He drew back, offended again. "You mean you *don't* think I'm good-looking?"

"Of course I do. You're handsome as hell—but you're only my fake groom, remember?"

"Oh, right." He stared at her strangely.

She couldn't figure out whether he was joking or not. "Is something wrong, Ross?"

"No…it's just I was wondering whether we'll be able to keep our heads through all of this."

"All of what?"

"You know, the wedding stuff." He gestured around the room as if it were a church packed to the gills with wedding guests.

Alison nodded. "I certainly know that *I* can keep my head."

"Oh, really?"

The way he was staring at her with those blue eyes of his made Alison very nervous. And very aware that she was telling a bald-faced lie. "Of course!"

A grin slashed crookedly across his lips. "Funny, you seemed a little peevish when I mentioned the divorce last night."

Now she was sure her cheeks were fiery red. "Well, naturally, when a man's kissing me, I don't want him to be thinking about divorce. How would you have felt if *I* had been the one who mentioned it?"

He actually seemed to consider her question for a moment. "Peeved, I guess—"

"There, you see?"

"—but glad you had the soundness of mind to remind me that ours is only going to be a short-term relationship," he finished.

Short-term. He made it sound as if they were going to have a fling or something. When really they were only getting married.

Nothing necessarily intimate about that.

She sat up straighter and squared her shoulders. "I suppose the solution to our worries is to simply not kiss each other."

"Why?"

She blinked. Did he *want* to kiss her again? She was tempted to find out—but temptation was precisely what they should be trying to avoid. "Because if we don't kiss each other, then we won't get carried away or be put into situations where either of us might have to hurt the other's feelings. Do you understand?"

He nodded, squinting at her in a thoughtful way. His eyes were so blue—the color of clear cool water. His gaze was intense, and she couldn't help noticing that the crinkly lines in his tanned skin as he squinted at her made him look even sexier. Only Ross would have devastating crow's-feet.

"That's a good idea," he agreed. "I think we should stick to it."

"To what?" she asked, still contemplating those eyes.

"No kissing."

She felt almost disappointed. He'd certainly gotten on board that idea quickly! She swallowed and looked away from him. "Good, then we're agreed."

He stood, stretching. "Yes. Of course we'll have to be very careful. Everyone will expect us to act like newlyweds."

"Okay, then, we'll give them a good show—but only in public."

He nodded, seeming satisfied. "Public displays of affection only," he repeated.

She looked up at him. He glanced down at her. Suddenly Alison realized she was sitting on the bed—something that seemed a little too intimate considering that they were in a room alone together and had just agreed to keep their distance. She hopped off it as if the mattress had turned to hot coals.

He smiled, and the silence stretched between them. Finally she cleared her throat.

He raised a rusty eyebrow. "Something wrong?"

"I'd...like to get dressed."

"Of course," he said. "I suppose I'll go downstairs, then."

She nodded and smiled until he'd backed out of the room. Just when she thought she was alone, he popped back in. "Don't forget Dad's having brunch downstairs."

"I won't."

This time he closed the door behind him. Relieved to be alone, Alison quickly took off her robe. There was so much to do she hardly knew where to begin. Of course, sometime soon she would have to start worrying about a wedding dress.

Just as she was halfway across the room to the bathroom, the door popped open again. Alison, absorbed in her own thoughts, nearly jumped out of her skin.

It was Ross. Grinning, he asked, "Handsome as hell, huh?"

And then he disappeared.

Ross was amazed by what resemblances people could discover when they were on the lookout for them.

Henry agreed wholeheartedly with the observation that the baby had Ross's nose. Also, Felicity, it turned out, had Henry's mouth, Alison's ears, Babs's naturally curving eyebrows and Alison's grandmother's shapely attractive knees—they looked like perfectly pudgy baby knees to Ross.

In spite of himself, he did feel his head swell a little with pride when they said Felicity looked like him, or when he held the baby up before her admiring fans. He'd never been around a baby for so long before. He'd always imagined they were all alike—it never occurred to him that each baby had its own strong personality that it started asserting as soon as it could grin or say goo-goo.

Felicity, for instance, didn't seem to mind being his daughter one bit. And she relished being the center of attention. The day before, his father had called Bea's Baby Boutique in town, and midmorning during brunch the truck arrived bearing a load of clothes, furniture, toys and stuffed animals. Henry must have cleaned the place out—and from the pleased imperialistic expression on Felicity's little face, Ross could tell the child believed she was finally getting the royal treatment she deserved.

Alison, on the other hand, appeared as though she would have gratefully crawled beneath a rock and stayed there. Every time someone so much as mentioned the wedding, she squirmed; when someone observed a likeness between Felicity and herself, she looked chagrined; and if ever Ross happened to touch her, she nearly rocketed out of her chair. But mostly, he noticed, she seemed bothered by her mother's talkativeness.

He couldn't really blame her for that. Babs kept up a running stream of nervous chatter, touching on everything from Alison's problems with diaper rash when she was a baby to the wedding that went awry one year earlier.

"Who said that rebound relationships don't work out?" Babs asked at one point over breakfast as she daintily stabbed a wedge of cantaloupe with her fork. "Alison must have met Ross just after her non-wedding last year." Her lips pursed into a pensive frown and she looked at Alison. "How old did you say Felicity was now?"

"Six months," Alison said, looking as if she would have gladly sunk through the carpet beneath her feet.

Babs did the math. Felicity would have been conceived three months before the wedding to Wes. Which meant that Alison *had* cheated on Wes. Her mouth opened in astonishment, then, thankfully, closed.

Silence ensued.

Henry cleared his throat. "Well, well, water under the bridge. The important thing is that the family is together at last."

"Hear! Hear!" Babs agreed, raising a mimosa glass. "True love conquers all."

Ross grinned like an idiot to cover his discomfort and stole an arm around Alison, who jumped. He gave her a bracing pat, shocked at how protective he felt toward the woman at his side. Though she sat stiff and upright in her chair, she looked brittle, vulnerable. He wished he could have spared her this; yet at the same time it seemed that her mother was finally coming to terms with her daughter making her own choices, leading her own life.

Of course, the life was a lie, but Babs didn't know that. Maybe in the end, the experience would prove useful for Alison.

If she managed to survive it.

He wished he could take her aside and tell her that

it would all be over soon. He also wanted to take her in his arms and tell her she was gorgeous, the most beautiful bride he ever could have hoped for, that even if he was only a fake groom, he had felt real jealousy at the idea of her talking on the phone to that creep Wes.

But they had agreed they wouldn't have any more private moments.

For some reason the prospect of not kissing Alison crushed him. He wasn't in love with her, exactly, but under different circumstances, he might have tried to pursue a relationship with her. He and Alison actually had a rapport, and despite her protests, they thought a lot alike. They were both businesspeople. They both were wary of getting involved. And now it felt like they had a history together.

He had to remind himself that their history only stretched back in hours, not years.

"Ross?"

Alison poked him in the ribs. Startled, Ross looked up and realized to his embarrassment that he had been staring at Alison.

"Look at them!" Babs exclaimed. "They can't take their eyes off each other!"

Ross glanced at his father. "You were saying?"

Henry chuckled. "I just wanted to make sure your tux was cleaned and pressed—for the wedding."

Ross nodded. Thanks to Hannah, his tuxedo was always at the ready. Henry's would be, too.

"I'm glad Henry told me about your plans when he asked me to fly out this morning, or I might not have had the presence of mind to bring a nice dress," Babs said.

Ross couldn't imagine Babs in anything *but* a nice

dress. The woman claimed to live in genteel poverty, but if she did, it was a kind of designer poverty kept up by the Neiman Marcus sales rack and trips to select outlet malls.

Alison went very still. Ross looked at her, wondering. Was she worried about what she would wear?

Sudden realization made him want to clap his hand on his forehead.

Of course! They had done so much worrying about other details about the wedding, almost everyone seemed to have forgotten about the bride—and that she might actually like to *look* like one!

Babs, noticing the lack of animation at the other side of the table, stared at her daughter and gasped. "Oh! Alison, I forgot to tell you. You don't have a thing to worry about. I brought your dress with me."

What little blood was left in Alison's cheeks soon drained out of them. "My...dress?"

"Why, your wedding dress of course," Babs said. "I've had it in its box for a year, honey. No sense letting it go to waste!"

"Oh, but, Mother—"

Before Alison could get in a word of protest, Hannah bustled into the room. "Looks like the first guests are arriving."

Henry looked up, curious. "But the wedding's not till two."

"The writing on the van says they're from Dallas," Hannah said.

"Dallas?" Babs was alert with interest at the mere mention of her hometown. "I wonder who it could be?"

Henry broke out in a huge grin. "This is the other surprise I had for Alison!" He screwed up his face comically and looked at Felicity. ''For you, too, sweetheart!''

He plucked Felicity out of her brand-new high chair and gestured for everyone to follow him out to the front porch. ''Come on, everyone! We must meet our honored guests—especially since Felicity is their namesake!''

The breakfast room emptied out as Ross, distracted by a groan, turned to Alison. She was rooted to her chair, still pale. ''Oh, Ross. I can't believe this is happening....''

''Are you worried about the dress?'' he asked. He could understand how she might not want to wear something that would remind her of a less-than-happy occasion in her life. ''It's only for one afternoon, then you'll never have to wear it again.''

She moaned. ''The dress! How could Mother have brought that here?''

''Well, you said she was trying to whisk you back into Wes's arms. Maybe she thought the dress would come in handy.''

Poor Alison. She'd only been awake for an hour, and she'd already been thrown for quite a few loops. Learning she would have to put on her long-ago wedding dress in a sort of reenactment of a day from her nightmares was probably a blow.

''Things just keep going from bad to worse,'' she moaned.

''Okay, so I can see that the dress is a problem. What else is so bad?''

''Don't you get it?'' Alison nodded toward the door the others had just exited through. ''The guests from Dallas, Felicity's namesake—it can only mean one thing.''

He looked at her questioningly, but instead of answering, she got up and led him to the front door. They arrived at the top step of the porch just in time to see the door to the van from St. Felicity's slide open and the nun he'd dealt with in Dallas pop out, followed by ten other nuns.

"Is that Sister...?" He couldn't remember the woman's name.

"Sister Joan," Alison finished, her mouth twisting wryly. "Also known as the hellion in Reeboks."

"I KNEW IT WOULD WORK. I knew it!"

Sister Joan bubbled over with enthusiasm for Alison's coming nuptials. Alison, who had sent her mother away and in the privacy of her bathroom was attempting to squeeze into her old wedding dress—the dreaded Wes dress—couldn't share her enthusiasm.

"What would work?" she asked. Surely not the side zipper that strained to the popping point as she attempted to slide it past her waist.

Naturally her question was ignored. Sister Joan tilted her head. "Which provided that extra encouragement—the purple one or the black?"

"I *knew* you had packed those on purpose!" Alison hollered. She stepped out of the bathroom—although she was careful to take baby steps and shallow breaths.

Sister Joan gaped at her. "Isn't that gown just a wee bit snug?" she asked just before popping one of Hannah's sand tarts into her mouth.

"I guess this is what comes of drowning one's sorrows in chocolate-chip cookies."

The nun laughed and popped another sand tart. "Oh, well," she said breezily, "I'm sure no one will notice."

Never mind that *she* had. Alison felt doom hovering over her. Then she looked into the full-length mirror at the corner of the room and could have wept. It was as if she was looking at a snapshot of herself from a year ago—only a year ago at this time she'd been happy. And about fifteen pounds thinner. She didn't know till later that Wes was going to dump her.

No, she'd been a starry-eyed optimist during the whole courtship, which even showed in her dress. She'd picked her wedding dress because it was one of those stylish sheath dresses, just like the movie stars wore, and that Bissett-Kennedy woman. Alison had had no inkling back then that by the time she actually did get some use out of the thing, she'd look less like a movie star than a satin sausage.

Feeling anxious, Alison downed a sand tart herself and sat on the edge of the bed, carefully.

"Oh, dear," Sister Joan said, scurrying over. "You don't look at all well. I hope your nerves hold out."

"I hope my seams hold out."

Sister Joan waved away her worries. "Nonsense. Who will notice?"

"Everyone will notice if I explode out of my casing like filling from an overbaked pastry."

The nun *tsk*ed at her. "The only one watching you closely will be Ross."

"Terrific."

"But, my dear, he loves you so—anyone can see that. He won't care if your dress looks...snug."

Alison wondered whether it was safe to tell Sister Joan the truth. Normally a nun would be a good bet to entrust with a secret, but Sister Joan was no ordinary nun.

"And of course, my dear, now that you are going

to be a Templeton, I hope you won't forget the convent."

"Now that I'm going to be a Templeton, it would be impossible to forget St. Felicity's, Sister. Especially since it was on their behalf that I was strong-armed into agreeing to Ross's scheme to begin with."

"Good!" Sister Joan said, blithely ignoring Alison's barbed tone. "Don't forget we've got that new day-care building going up. Buildings cost money, you know."

This from the woman who had already squeezed twenty thousand dollars out of her would-be fiancé. "Don't you think you ought to wait a while before hitting Ross up for money again?"

"Of course, I wouldn't dream of asking him," Sister Joan said, looking almost offended. "That's why I'm asking you."

"Even if I did want to give St. Felicity's money, I couldn't. I don't have any money. I'm not a Templeton."

"But you will be, dear. Ross will be your husband, and what's his will be yours, etcetera, etcetera. It says so in the scriptures!"

Alison rolled her eyes. Sister Joan *would* quote the Bible when it came to extorting money from people. That was the last straw. "I don't mean to burst your bubble, Sister, but Ross won't be my husband. He doesn't love me, either. He's only marrying me because back when we thought his father was dying, we told him we were getting married. When we realized that he was well, neither of us had the nerve to confess the truth."

Sister Joan seemed to deflate before her very eyes. "Oh." She sighed. "So the purple one didn't work?"

"I'm afraid not." She shook her head, remembering the way Ross had been looking at her this morning in this very room. Maybe it had worked...a little.

"Shoot."

Alison let out a long breath. "By the new year, I'll probably be back to being plain old Alison Bennett again. And it will be a relief, believe me."

"So you're going to get a divorce right after the wedding?" Sister Joan asked.

"Maybe not right after," Alison said. She didn't want to divorce so quickly that their motives would be clear to Henry and her mother. If they ever discerned the truth, she would feel really underhanded. "We might wait a few months."

"Oh." Sister Joan thought for a moment, then looked at Alison seriously. "You know we don't condone divorce."

Alison nodded. "I know. I'm sorry." Here came the guilt again.

"As well you should be," Sister Joan said. Then she slanted a conspiratorial look Alison's way. "But if you give a little for the day care, Sister Catherine might see her way around to asking the bishop to give you an annulment—"

"Sister Joan!" Alison cried, horrified that she was being blackmailed by a nun.

Then again, considering who she was dealing with, why should she have been surprised?

Sister Joan cackled with glee. "Just joking, just joking."

"I should hope so." But she wasn't so sure.

A knock sounded at the door, and Alison took as deep a breath as her dress would allow, trying to gear herself up mentally to deal with her mother, and her mother's reaction to her ill-fitting wedding gown.

"Alison, it's me."

Alison sat up. "It's Ross!"

Sister Joan nodded, but didn't budge. "I heard."

Apparently she wasn't going to offer to make herself scarce. Alison stood carefully and crossed to the door, which she cracked open a smidgen and peeked her head through. Ross stood before her, smiling. He was still in his jeans and was carrying a large yellowed clothing box and a smaller round box of the same vintage.

"I just realized I haven't given you a wedding present," he said.

"But you don't—"

He shoved the box toward her, cutting off her words. "I thought you might like to try this on for size. I asked Dad, and he thought it was a good idea."

Alison frowned, but she had to admit that her curiosity was piqued. "All right," she said, taking the boxes.

What could be in them?

Before she could ask Ross any of the questions burning in her mind, he was already halfway down the hall.

Alison closed the door and walked back to the bed, where she opened the clothing box. Its contents made her gasp in delight.

It had to be Ross's mother's wedding dress.

She broke the seal covering the dress and picked it up carefully. The silk was a creamy color, and the dress was elegantly cut. The collar was a simple yoke, both in front and in back, where a hundred little silk-covered buttons marched down to the dress's narrow waist. The skirt was full, and in the tissue paper beneath the dress was a tulle petticoat, along with elbow-length gloves that matched the fabric of the dress.

Sister Joan opened the round box and pulled out a perfectly adorable hat, which was little more than a silk skull cap, except that it was lined with velvet piping and had a jaunty little veil attached.

The whole ensemble looked like something Grace Kelly might have worn.

"Surely he doesn't want me to wear this!" Alison said in awe, as if the outfit actually *had* belonged to Grace Kelly. After all, the dress was bound to have sentimental value to Henry. She already felt like an impostor, but in the heirloom wedding gown...

"Well, of course he does," Sister Joan, ever the practical one, said. "Why else would he have shown it to you? He's trying to save you the humiliation of wearing that thing you have on."

Alison's eyes teared up. It was such a sweet thing for him to have offered her! He must have sensed how horrified she'd been by her mother's showing up with the Wes dress. He'd come to her rescue.

But no doubt he was only doing it because he was a kind person, and because he was grateful to her for doing him a favor. It didn't mean that he had any sort of tender feelings for her.

Sister Joan perched the hat atop Alison's head and twirled her around to see the effect in the full-length mirror. "Very sweet!" the nun exclaimed.

It was perfect. All her hesitations about wearing the dress melted away.

"Say what you will, the man loves you."

"No, he doesn't." Alison couldn't allow herself to

think that. She was already looking forward much too much to being Ross's wife, for however brief a time.

"Maybe he just doesn't know it yet," Sister Joan said as Alison disappeared into the bathroom again to try on the dress. "But if he ever does know it, you might mention to him that St. Felicity's could use a billiard table, too."

Alison poked her head out the door and looked at the nun dubiously. "A billiard table?"

Sister Joan's eyes widened, all innocence. "For our new youth rec center, of course."

Chapter Nine

When the music started, Alison's heartbeat tripped as if she was actually getting married. Maybe because she actually was. The ceremony would be real, even if the sentiment behind it wasn't.

Sensing her nervousness, Henry turned to her with a smile. In a tux, he looked dapper and yet still jolly—like Santa decked out for a madcap night in Manhattan. "You're beautiful, Alison."

They paused at the top of the staircase. "It was so wonderful of you to let me wear Ross's mother's dress."

His smile disappeared for just the briefest of moments before returning full force. "It's a pleasure to see it again—almost like having Anita back again."

Anita. So that was Ross's mother's name. And as she looked at Henry, and the emotion the name had stirred in him, she felt the familiar wave of guilt. This ceremony might mean nothing to her and Ross, but for their parents, it was the real thing. Wasn't that part of the reason she'd agreed to go through with the wedding to begin with?

Now her good intentions seemed less than honorable—especially when she got a load of the horde of people awaiting them at the bottom of the staircase. They were all standing, smiling at Henry and eyeing her with great interest, the bride who had precipitated such a lavish spur-of-the-moment affair. Alison's knees went rubbery and she leaned more heavily on Henry's arm.

"Courage," he said to her through his smile, as smoothly as a ventriloquist.

She looked ahead through the small aisle they had cleared between the chairs in the parlor and spotted Ross. Although his lips were quirked into a kind of smile, he appeared as nervous as she was. Even so, he was handsomer than ever, almost sinfully so. The black-and-white lines of his tux emphasized his incredible build and lent him an air of Cary Grant sophistication. As she gazed into his devastating blue eyes, Alison suddenly felt as though she were walking on Jell-O.

"Smile," Henry said, almost without moving his lips. "This is the day you've been waiting your whole life for."

"Of course," she said, not letting the irony through. The day she'd been waiting for? *The day she entered into a bogus marriage with a man she barely knew?*

Somehow, the thought did make her smile. She looked again at Ross, whose own expression had turned completely serious. Was he regretting their decision not to tell Henry the truth? Her heart skittered in her chest. Maybe he felt the same guilt she did for lying to his father this way. In which case, what was to prevent him from calling off the wedding?

By the time Henry stopped her in front of the preacher, with the still-unsmiling Ross at her side, she felt positively sick. Pastor Wilkins began the ceremony, and Alison fought to pay attention, but the somewhat familiar words were a whir in her ears. Out of the corner of her eye she kept scoping out the nearest exit. That way, when the preacher asked if there were any objections to the marriage and Ross made the humiliating public confession that this was all just a sham to cover the fact that they were a pair of lying cowards, she would know exactly where to run. Her biggest regret was that she had borrowed a pair of her mother's pumps and not Sister Joan's Reeboks.

Out of the recesses of her consciousness, the preacher intoned, "And now if anyone can show just cause why..."

Alison's mind snapped back to the matter at hand. Next to her, Ross gave her arm a soft squeeze and her heart thumped ominously in her chest. *The jig was up.* Soon she would be making a dash for the door, and the guests behind her would be lobbing Hannah's sand tarts and little radish roses from the vegetable plate at her back.

But the moment passed and the cleric droned on. Ross's grip on her arm loosened, and Alison's heartbeat returned to something like normal. Except that she was still nervous. And she still had her heel firmly dug into the rug, like a sprinter at the starting line.

Suddenly, in response to something Pastor Wilkins had said, Ross took her hand in his, and before she knew what was happening, a gold band with five diamonds embedded in it was thrust onto her ring finger.

Alison sucked in her breath, looking at her finger in a daze. *Ross had bought her a wedding ring?*

"...as long as you both shall live?"

Alison blinked, recognizing her cue.

So soon? She opened her mouth to respond, but her

throat felt as if she had swallowed a bag of cotton balls.

Ross nudged her and she coughed out her reply. "...do!"

Murmured laughter sounded behind her, and when a thicker solid gold band was thrust into her hand by his father, she shoved it onto Ross's finger nervously.

In the next moment Ross heard his vows and said a solid "I do." And then the preacher pronounced them husband and wife and Ross pulled her into his arms and kissed her on the mouth.

Alison's head was swimming with emotion—relief that the first big hurdle had been cleared, dread about the reception to come, and confusion, because the official end-of-ceremony kiss Ross was bestowing on her was developing into something that would be more appropriate behind closed doors. And they had both agreed that nothing of that sort was ever to take place.

Finally he released her, and she stepped away with a gasp as the air whooshed back into her lungs. She weaved dizzily and barely heard more murmured laughter behind them just before the music started up and they marched to the back of the room to the familiar Mendelssohn strains. They anchored themselves at the end of one of the banquet tables loaded down with goodies and prepared to receive their guests.

It seemed like Henry had invited half of Texas. Her arm fairly ached from shaking the hands of well-wishers, none of whom she knew, except for the sisters of St. Felicity's, whose black-and-white habits made them stand out in the crowd. At Ross's right was Babs, and every time someone congratulated her on her daughter's marriage, she blurted, "Isn't it wonderful?

She's just made me the happiest mom-in-law in the world."

And after a day at the Templeton home, Alison could certainly see why. The bounty of wealth all around never ceased to amaze her. After one simple phone call, her baby had more clothes and toys than did all the babies she worked with combined. In a mere day the house had undergone the transformation from a sick man's residence to a party palace, thanks to a swarm of servants who seemingly stood at the ready for just such an occasion. All Alison had to do was ask for something, and it was done. If she was thirsty, Hannah would reel off a list of beverages for her to choose from. Living in the Templeton house was probably not too distant an experience from staying at one of their swankier hotels.

This aspect of the marriage probably most appealed to Babs. That, and as a connoisseur of physical beauty, she could hardly fail to appreciate Ross. Alison herself felt lucky to be standing next to him as his fake wife—perhaps luckier than his real wife would have been. She imagined a woman married to Ross for real would find it hard to relax with such a good-looking husband.

Especially if he made a habit of bestowing toe-curling kisses like the one he'd given her at the altar. Those especially she would guard jealously.

"You're holding up beautifully," Ross whispered to her. "Just a few more hours and this will all be over."

Hours. She couldn't wait. Ross handed her some champagne. "The handshaking's over, so we can relax a little."

Says he, she thought, taking the glass and a slug

from it. The taste was smooth and the bubbliness of it tickled her nose.

She turned to him, discreetly motioning with her ring finger. "It's so beautiful, Ross—you shouldn't have."

His blue eyes looked into hers for a moment, then he shrugged. "No big deal. We had to get the props right."

Props. Alison looked down at her wedding ring and felt equal parts regret and awe. What a prop! It was probably the most expensive thing she'd ever owned. But then she didn't really own it. This was all pretend.

Just as Alison was taking another bracing gulp of champagne, Henry held a glass of bubbly in his hand and tapped an ornate silver spoon against it to get everyone's attention.

When the room was quiet, he began, "I'd like to propose a toast. Just two days ago I thought my life might be coming to an end. Then one morning, I received more good news in three hours than most men receive in a lifetime. First I had my health. Then my son brought me my adorable little granddaughter, Felicity. And finally he told me that he was going to be married to Felicity's mother. And so this is my toast—to my daughter-in-law, Alison Bennett Templeton, who has made me the *second*-happiest man in the world today."

Alison felt all eyes on her and wanted to sink through the floor. A smile so stiff she feared her mouth would crack spread across her face, and she took another swig of champagne, careful not to look at Ross for fear of giving away their secret.

"But enough talking—it's time for the bride and groom to dance," Henry announced.

That was another tradition she had forgotten about. She hadn't noticed a band setting up, but the same trio of violin, bass and piano that had played the wedding march now launched into an easy rendition of "All I Do Is Dream of You."

Ross was apparently more prepared. Without missing a beat, he gathered her into his arms and danced her into the marble-floored foyer that served as a ballroom.

Alison felt swept off her feet. And in Ross's strong arms that was definitely a pleasurable feeling. Much too pleasurable.

"You dance divinely," she quipped, trying to lighten the tension between them.

He grinned devilishly. "Never had a lesson."

"Somehow that doesn't surprise me."

He cocked a brow as he twirled them around the room. "Why not?"

She lifted her shoulders. "Maybe because you seem like the type of man to whom all of life's gifts come easily."

He laughed. "Why, because I'm rich?"

She nodded. "Rich and good-looking and you were probably a whiz in school, too. Am I right?"

"Not quite. I was a gangly kid with braces, my first choice for a date to the junior prom turned me down cold, and I flunked algebra the first time and had to take it over in summer school."

She regarded him skeptically, trying hard to visualize him as an ugly duckling. It didn't work. "Let me guess. Your braces actually came off early, your first choice for a date to the prom was head varsity cheerleader, and the summer school instructor turned out to be a beautiful math-loving coed who took one look at you, tore off her glasses and let down her hair, and ended up giving you an A."

He tossed back his head and laughed again. "You're almost right. My *second* choice was head varsity cheerleader."

No telling who his first choice was; Alison didn't doubt she was off-the-charts popular. And just as good-looking as Ross probably was, no matter what he said.

That afternoon Alison danced more than she had in her entire life. The whole day was a whirl of strange faces, enthusiastic chitchat about how happy she was and one glass of champagne after another. Her glass was bottomless; unfortunately her tolerance wasn't. By the time someone hauled her over to the big banquet table to cut the four-layer bride's cake there, she was definitely feeling a little tipsy. And after telling so many people how happy she was to be Mrs. Templeton, she almost believed she *was* Ross's loving wife.

She met her hubby behind the cake and gave him a big wet kiss. When he pulled away, he eyed her with raised-brow interest. "Say, how many have you had?"

She grinned. "Who's counting?"

It took her three tries to shove a piece of cake into his mouth in front of the crowd and flashing cameras. She was wiping the white icing off his lips when his father started banging his glass again in preparation for another announcement.

"I thought now would be the perfect time to announce my gift to the newlyweds."

Ross and Alison looked at each other, startled. She hadn't expected Henry to give them anything, and apparently neither had he.

"Dad, you shouldn't—"

Henry laughed, cutting him off. "I might be the only one who's noticed, but these two haven't said a durn thing about taking a honeymoon. So I've ordered the lodge in Colorado opened up and put at their disposal for the next week."

Everyone oohed and ahhed as Ross and Alison gaped at each other. A *honeymoon?* The idea was sobering. A week of being holed up in a lodge with Ross for a week, trying to keep her end of the no-kissing bargain, sounded more torturous than a week at St. Felicity's.

Which reminded her...

"Ross, I can't leave Felicity for a whole week." She raised her brows, remembering suddenly that she had other obligations. "I can't leave my work for a week, either. I've already been gone too long."

Ross nodded. "You don't have to tell me. I've got to catch a plane to Switzerland tomorrow."

She crossed her arms, amazed. "You're going to Switzerland the day after our wedding?" She knew she shouldn't be annoyed. But she was.

"I didn't know we were getting married. Besides... you know."

Right. It wasn't a real marriage. "Isn't your father going to think that's a little funny, your leaving me so soon?"

Ross grinned. "You wanna come?"

Switzerland? "Of course not!" After she blurted the knee-jerk retort, she thought again. Switzerland...with Ross...newlyweds.... "Absolutely not," she said, struggling to hold on to her composure.

He nodded. "Don't worry. We'll talk to Dad."

As soon as people started piling into line for the

cake, Alison and Ross cornered Henry and took him into the library.

"We can't thank you enough for the offer of the house in Colorado, Dad," Ross began. "But Alison and I both feel we can't leave Felicity."

His father grinned. "Nonsense. Felicity can stay right here with me."

Alison and Ross exchanged glances. This argument wasn't going to work as well as they had hoped.

"But you see," Ross went on, "we've just come together as a family, and it would be hard to be separated right now."

Henry remained unflappable. "But right now is precisely when you should be separated! Two people just married need to get off by themselves for a while to unwind, and you can't unwind with a little baby in tow. Heaven's sake—now that I have one grandchild, I'd like to think there might be some others along the way. Felicity's not going to get a little brother or sister if you're always worn out at the end of the day from tending to her."

Alison was certain her face was on fire. "But, Henry, Felicity is a real handful. Are you sure you're up to having her here?"

He looked astonished. "A handful? Felicity? She's a little angel! Between Hannah, Babs and myself, we should manage fine."

Babs? "My mother?" Alison practically squeaked.

"I've asked her to stay at the ranch for a while," Henry said. "Got to get acquainted with my new family, you know."

Alison didn't want her mother staying with Henry—what if the two of them started piecing together inconsistencies in their kids' lives? And she didn't want to leave Felicity, either. It wasn't that she had become really attached to the child, but she had promised Sister Joan to look after Felicity.

And in spite of the fact that Felicity had been perfectly content for almost an entire day now, how could she be sure that would last? What if Felicity got upset? What if she cried?

That unfamiliar stabbing sensation struck her heart again.

"Do you know any oldies?" she asked Henry, as if interviewing him for a nanny's position.

"Most all my friends could be called oldies," he said, not catching her drift.

"I mean rock groups. The Beatles. The Beach Boys. The Stones."

"Alison..." Ross apparently felt uncomfortable with this form of inquiry and sensed its futility. "I'm sure Hannah would help out."

Whose side was he on? "Hannah looks like she would be more into Bing Crosby than Crosby, Stills and Nash."

"Who wouldn't?" Ross asked.

"Felicity," Alison reminded him. "Felicity's never been away from me. What if something goes wrong?"

He looked at her as if she had lost her mind—much the same way she was looking at him. Had he forgotten that they were *not* supposed to go on a honeymoon?

"We've got to leave her sometime, darling."

"And what about my work?"

Henry frowned. "You're working while Felicity's so young?"

Alison suddenly felt as if she were in another dimension. A week ago she would never have believed she would be standing in the library of a Western-style mansion, trying to talk her husband out of going on a honeymoon while her new father-in-law lectured her about being a working mother. She had definitely stepped into the domestic Twilight Zone.

"Ross, can I speak to you for a minute?" she asked.

Henry jumped out of his chair. "Let me get out of your way. You two will have a lot to talk about." He left them alone, then ducked his head back in the door and said, "But I do hope you'll take me up on my lodge offer." He frowned. "It seems peculiar, a man and a woman, just married, who don't want to be alone."

He ducked back out again.

Ross looked at Alison for a long moment, searing her with the brilliant intensity of those blue eyes. "He's right. It *does* seem odd."

"Then you think we should go?" Alison asked, amazed. "What about my business? What about your appointment in Switzerland?"

"This is more important to me," Ross said. "This is family."

Which Alison translated as: He had already invested a lot of emotional capital in fooling his father into believing they were married. He didn't want to blow it now.

"When does it end?" Alison asked. When he merely stared at her blankly, she went on, "To what lengths are we supposed to go to keep carrying on this charade?"

He was silent for a long moment. "The honeymoon's just for a week," he said finally, offering no answer to her question.

"A week!" Alison exclaimed. If there was anything

she'd learned in the past year, not to mention since she'd known Ross, it was that the course of a mere day could turn life topsy-turvy. A week? No telling what could happen!

Especially since during that one week she would be alone with Ross in a lodge in the mountains of Colorado. Off-season. What else would they be able to think about besides sex?

At least, she knew that was what *she* would be thinking about.

"Wouldn't your mother find it peculiar if you went right back to work after getting married?" Ross asked.

Her mother!

Peculiar? Babs would think it was downright bizarre and start worrying about her precarious status as in-law to the well-heeled. Alison wouldn't put anything past her. Babs might even hire private detectives to follow Ross. If she discovered anything amiss, she could become fixated on Wes again.

That was it. If there was any benefit to herself in her fake marriage, it was that her mother had finally come to terms with the Wes situation. She didn't want to do anything to jeopardize that.

"What's the weather like in Colorado?" she asked.

Ross smiled.

That smile made her nervous. She was afraid it would be her undoing someday. "This is just about family," she reminded him. "We're still going to abide by our no-physical-involvement pledge. Right?"

The smile broadened. "It's just about family," he agreed.

He didn't say a thing about the pledge.

"I'LL BUY A HOTEL," Ross said.

He reached across the board and slapped a little red

plastic piece onto Park Place.

''You *would* buy a hotel.'' Alison scowled. ''That's so unfair!''

As if in agreement, the heavens sent down an angry bolt of lightning. It had rained all evening. Rained and rained and rained. After their late arrival, Alison and Ross had eaten the sumptuous feast laid out for them by the shoestring staff, then rattled around the empty lodge for an hour. The electricity had gone out, so there was no television to watch. The only light came from candles and the embers in the fireplace, so snuggling into a quiet corner wasn't advisable, either.

What were two people on their honeymoon in an empty candlelit lodge supposed to do?

Of course, Ross knew what he would like to do: pull Alison into his arms and kiss her until the rain stopped beating at the windowpanes, which from the looks of things, might be never. He couldn't say precisely when his weakness for Alison had finally gotten the best of him. Maybe it was when her mother had told her she'd brought the old wedding dress and he'd realized how glad he was that she hadn't married Wes. Or maybe it was when the preacher pronounced them husband and wife. Or maybe it was when she'd been so eager to avoid going on the honeymoon, and he'd looked into her eyes and realized the reason—she was afraid that *she* wouldn't be able to keep their no-intimacy pledge.

He grinned. ''Your turn.''

Alison grumbled and rolled the dice, landing herself safely on a piece of property he didn't own. He took his turn barely thinking about the game, which he had suggested as a way to keep Alison from running off to her room and calling it a night, which she had threatened to do.

He didn't know why he was torturing himself, since he knew getting involved with Alison would be a mistake. Hadn't she told him all along that he was just the type of man she didn't want?

He wished she would relax a little bit, maybe have some fun. It was strange; at first he'd thought he was only physically attracted to her. Now he found that he enjoyed just being around her. Her brittleness and self-effacing humor amused him and made him feel protective toward her. He wished he could convince her that all men weren't like Wes. And especially not himself, no matter what outward similarities he might share with that creep.

Alison moved her little dog and groaned. "'Go to jail!'"

He laughed. "You seem to have a knack for that."

"Believe it or not, I had never even seen a jail before I hooked up with you."

"Stick with me, baby," he drawled. "I'll take you to all the best places. Switzerland, Colorado..."

"The county detention center..." Her smile finally broke into laughter. One mission accomplished, he thought. He knew he should probably let it end there. What purpose could getting involved with this woman right now possibly serve?

The trouble was, he'd let Alison think he was just using her to convince his dad he was a grandpa, when the truth was actually much more complicated. He was attracted to Alison. He wanted her. And even though he had carefully guarded his bachelorhood for these past thirty-five years, he didn't even mind being married to her.

She slid her dog into the jail box and leaned back in her chair. "Just my luck that I'd be spending my wedding night behind bars."

The flickering candles seemed to highlight all the beautiful lines of her face. Her strong jaw, her slightly upturned nose, her gorgeous cheekbones. Ross, who would have been happy to simply bask in her beauty, had to remind himself that he was expected to keep up one side of the conversation. He blurted out the first thing that came into his head.

"Where were you supposed to go on your honeymoon with Wes?"

Her face fell, almost as if he'd mentioned ptomaine poisoning. Ross could have kicked himself.

"Florida."

He imagined the hopping nightlife of Miami, white sand beaches, Alison in a bikini strolling arm in arm…with another man. Wishing he'd never brought up the subject, he said inanely, "I've always liked beaches."

Alison barked out a laugh. "Me, too. But Wes hated them."

"Then why were you going to Florida?"

"Because there was a golf course in St. Petersburg Wes had never been to. He was a big golfer."

"Are you?"

She wrinkled her nose. "Can't stand it. I was supposed to be a spectator."

Ross felt his jaw drop. "You mean the man wanted to spend his honeymoon playing golf, which you didn't even like to play?"

She giggled. "Stupid, huh? I suppose there were signs that things might not work out between us…if I had been looking for them."

"I'd say a one-sided golfing honeymoon could be considered more than a sign," Ross observed. "A billboard, maybe."

"Another was the fact that he didn't even ask me before booking the reservations. Stupid me, I was so bowled over by the prospect of becoming the man's wife, I didn't even consider telling him what I really wanted to do."

"What was that?" Ross asked.

She shrugged. "I suppose it's silly, but ever since I was a little girl, I've always dreamed of going to Hawaii on my honeymoon. It always sounded so exotic and beautiful. I imagined being on some remote part of the island near a breathtakingly beautiful sand beach, in a cozy little bungalow. Probably drinking champagne out of a coconut shell...you know, the whole tropical-paradise bit."

"And who was your dream groom?" he asked, curious.

Two splotches of color dotted Alison's cheeks. She shrugged. "Don Ho, I guess. When you're a little girl, it doesn't seem to matter that much, so long as the setting's right."

"And when you're an adult?"

Her lips parted, but no sound came out. He had the most devilish impulse to lean across the Monopoly board and plant a kiss on those perfect lips of hers.

"When you're an adult you learn to settle for golfing in Florida," she said finally.

She was trying to joke, but he could see she was speaking from her heart, which was still stinging from Wes's rebuff. "You shouldn't have to settle, Alison. Not for a golfing trip or—"

His words cut off abruptly and she grinned, her

white teeth flashing in the candlelight. "Or a lodge in the Rockies?"

"I'm sorry," he said.

"Why?" She shrugged again. "I probably would have needed a break after this weekend, especially after that week in the convent."

"I meant, I'm sorry Wes turned out to be such a jerk. I'm sorry you've given up on the idea of marriage."

She laughed. "After today some people might say I've embraced it."

There was that humor again, providing a safe wedge between them.

She leaned back and for a moment Ross worried that her rocker might turn clean over. "Besides, I haven't met anyone the least bit interested in me since Wes."

He leaned forward and took her hand. "Haven't you?"

She attempted to draw away, but he held her fast. "You're breaking the agreement, Ross," she said in the same voice she'd used when he'd put the hotel on Park Place. "We made a deal that this was to be a no-touching kind of marriage."

"That's just as good a defense as a nun's habit, isn't it?"

Alison blinked.

"Alison..." He wasn't sure what he wanted to propose to her. A not-so-platonic marriage? An indefinite stay of their divorce plans? A date?

It didn't matter. Before he could utter another syllable, she launched herself out of her chair and galloped for the nearest phone. "I think we should check on Felicity, don't you?"

He frowned. "Are the phone lines back up?"

They had been down about an hour before.

She picked up the receiver of the old-fashioned table phone and listened for a dial tone. Her face lit up. "Eureka!" she said, her finger already swinging around the rotary dial at breakneck speed. "I hope she's all right. Thank goodness for Hannah. Between your father and my mother, Felicity would probably be living on cookies and cake for the entire week."

She drummed her fingers for a few moments as she waited for someone at the other end to pick up. Finally she stopped, exclaiming, "Henry! This is Alison. We were just calling to check on Felicity. How is she?"

Her eyes widened and she looked up at Ross. Her frown sent him scurrying over.

"You don't think she's sick, do you?" Alison said. She lifted the receiver up and a little away from her ear so Ross could hear the response. He could also hear Felicity's familiar cries in the background. Being so far away, unable to help, made his heart almost ache.

"I don't think so," Henry said. "We've already had a doctor here to check her out."

"And what did he say?" Ross asked, alarmed.

"That she's fit as a fiddle. Hannah thinks she just misses her mommy and daddy, but I'll be darned if this baby of yours isn't just in a very bad mood."

Ross and Alison exchanged knowing glances.

"You better put her on the phone, Dad," Ross told his father.

"You mean Felicity?"

"We can take care of this," Alison assured him.

Henry let out a doubtful grunt, but they heard him walking with the portable phone to another part of the house and sitting down. Felicity's lusty sobs grew louder and louder. Alison held the phone farther away from her ear and looked up at Ross.

"Okay, here she is," came the faraway sound of Henry's voice.

"What do you think?" Alison whispered to Ross. "Marvin Gaye again?"

Ross thought for a moment, then told her, "Follow me." He launched into the first stanza of "Stand by Me," which immediately made Alison smile. She began a modest doo-wop accompaniment, and they leaned into the phone together, close, trying to hear if their song was having the desired effect.

Sure enough, Felicity's cries became intermittent, and they began to sing more softly, making the jaunty tune into a soulful lullaby. Ross put his arm around Alison's waist, and she looked up at him just as she was singing to her darling, darling to stand by her. Suddenly they both seemed to realize that, literally, he was standing just as close as physically possible. And that their lips were just inches apart.

The song trailed off into the night, leaving them huddled together, staring deeply into each other's eyes, the phone forgotten.

After a few moments Henry's faint tinny voice could be heard. "That's wonderful! She's fallen asleep."

Alison smiled. Ross felt his lips curling up in response. He swallowed. Her gaze darted down to his Adam's apple, then back up to his lips, where it seemed to hit a snag. She wet her own lips with her tongue, making them seem impossibly moist and inviting. Ross felt himself bend a fraction. Or maybe it was Alison who had tilted her face up.

"Ross? Alison?" the faraway voice asked. "Are you still there?"

Just barely. The voice came to Ross's fuzzy consciousness like an alarm clock attempting to wake him from a dream. But he was loath to give up this dream, especially when it was so tantalizingly real, so soft in his arms....

He took the phone from Alison's hand. "Night, Dad," he said in the general direction of the receiver. He dropped the receiver and could tell by its noisy clatter that he'd missed the target of returning it to its cradle. And remedying the mistake was the furthest thing from his mind.

He hauled Alison into his arms and kissed her like there was no tomorrow.

Chapter Ten

Alison, who had kept her desires in check so successfully for so long, sank into his arms as willingly and irreversibly as a pagan maiden surrendering herself to the fire gods. The feeling inside her wasn't too far off from having hurled herself into a volcano, either. She had lost her bearings, lost all sense of time, lost all the reserve that had shielded her emotions for so long. The only thing she was conscious of was being in Ross's strong arms, the fire in the hearth and various candles, casting a warm glow over the dark stone room with its oak ceiling beams, and the undeniable truth that she wanted Ross every bit as much as he apparently wanted her.

That last feeling had nothing to do with the fact that they were married. And little to do with the fact that she had repressed every sexual urge she'd had since Wes had defected. It had everything to do with the fact that she was wildly attracted to Ross, the last man on earth she'd planned on falling for.

She'd worried that his smile would be her undoing. Instead, it had been his smoldering gaze. That, and his deep voice crooning "Stand by Me" in her ear when she was already practically standing in his lap.

He shifted, slanting his mouth across hers at a whole new angle, and for a moment, they were consumed in this new configuration of lips. She lifted her hands and ran her fingers up the strong lines of his jaw, then through his hair, then settled them at the nape of his neck, where she clung to him and drew herself closer, moving her body suggestively against his.

He understood the suggestion perfectly. As the kiss deepened, involving an intricate mating dance of their tongues, Ross massaged her—her shoulders, down her back, lingering on her hips and then pulling her so close she could feel his maleness pressing into her. A moan escaped her lips.

It wasn't just that it had been forever since she'd been with a man. The wonderful ache inside her seemed all about Ross, an emotional response to his caring about her.

It was crazy. They barely knew each other.

But Lord, he felt so good. And she needed this closeness, this loving touch he was so willingly bestowing on her.

And, after all, they *were* married.

Her need grew more frenzied, and just as she began considering how to invite her new husband to her bedroom for the night, she realized they were moving, sinking down to something soft.

An imitation but very real-feeling black bearskin rug broke their free fall and cradled them as they worked with zippers and undid buttons with trembling fingers. Alison removed Ross's shirt and gasped as she revealed the fabulous sinewy muscles of his arms and chest. She remembered thinking he had an incredible body when she'd seen him shirtless in the hotel room. Now she felt like the proverbial kid in a candy shop.

And the most amazing thing was, Ross seemed as delighted with her as she was with him. Never before had she known a man to take his time undressing her, making every separate button a new erotic experience. She had a craving to feel her bare body next to his, but each time he uncovered another few inches of her skin and lovingly sampled it with a kiss or flick of the tongue, she understood the rewards of patience.

When finally he had removed her shirt, he paused for a moment, his appreciative loving gaze making her blush to the core. "You're beautiful," he whispered. "Perfect."

As he said the last word, his gaze moved up and met hers, as if daring her to come back with a denial or a quip. She remained silent, amazed by the sincerity in his tone.

His searing gaze burned a fiery path right down to her soul. She couldn't deny how much she wanted him, and more, how much she wanted to believe every word he said to her and wanted to endow his every touch with emotion. Desire. Caring. Love. She'd been in need of all those things for such a long time.

He placed his hands on her hips and she lifted her lips to his again. "Ross, I want you to love me."

This time when their lips touched again, she sensed she had finally tapped out all of Ross's patience. He moved against her needfully and sank down to lie flush against the rug, pulling her on top of him. In that moment the whole world seemed to be contained in this one room, lit with the golden glow of firelight, with just the two of them.

Slowly his hands pushed her skirt up to her hips and began to massage her thighs and the most sensitive part of her. She let out a gentle moan again, moving on top of him. She had never felt such desire. Such heat building in her. His gaze blazed into hers, and she leaned down until their bodies were length-to-length and with her hand began to massage his own sensitive male flesh.

"Alison..." he growled in warning.

She smiled, continuing her tender ministrations.

In a sudden movement he rolled and hovered just over her, his body seeming to cover hers protectively. Strange, she had known him for such a short time, but in this moment she trusted him completely. She felt safe.

She lifted her hips to meet him, and when he entered her, it was as if the whole world had stopped for them. Nothing had ever felt so right to her before. She gave a sigh of pure pleasure.

A sure and yet utterly tender smile worked across his lips, and he began to move inside her, slowly bringing her desire to the boiling point. She felt like putty in his hands, and yet was shocked to find how much power her own desire had over him. When finally their mutual need spiraled out of control and exploded in a burst of fire, Alison experienced that free-falling sensation again. But this time the delicious feeling seemed to go on and on, as if she would never touch ground again. And she never wanted to.

SUNLIGHT STREAMED IN through the curtains onto her face. Even in her sleep Alison could sense the bright warmth and squinted her eyes against it. She stretched and yawned, taking inventory of every sore muscle in her body—and there were many. She smiled, having a vague memory that she'd acquired her aches and pains in the most pleasurable way possible. Except that her back was killing her. Now what could have caused that?

She turned and realized that she was lying on something soft that in turn rested on a very hard surface. She peeked through one partially opened eyelid and saw, to her horror, a grinning beast staring straight at her.

With a yelp she shot up to a sitting position, adrenaline coursing through her veins. From her new vantage point, she saw that the animal who had been watching her was merely the fake head of the imitation bear rug. What a silly thing to be afraid of! She let out a breath of relief, until she realized that she had slept the whole night on a bearskin rug with Ross, who like herself, was still stark naked. Her face reddened as she took stock. One of his arms was draped possessively over her left calf, which indicated to her that they must have fallen asleep at some point with their heads on opposite ends of the bear.

She looked down at Ross—handsome, gloriously naked, with the same wicked satisfied grin on his lips that had probably been playing across hers moments before she awoke. Would his disappear when the full realization of what they had done last night occurred to him?

No doubt. She was appalled. One minute they had been playing Monopoly—and what could be safer than that?—and the next moment she had been begging him to make love to her. *She* had been begging. That fact stunned her.

She just wasn't the type of woman who had dalliances. And yet she had jumped onto the bearskin rug with Ross wholeheartedly, with very little encouragement, knowing full well the million-plus reasons she should have stayed miles away from him. The past year she had been practically numb with heartbreak, yet here she was, putting herself—and her heart—in jeopardy.

What on earth could she have been thinking?

Of course she *hadn't* been thinking, that was the problem. Instead, she had behaved as if she were nothing but a bundle of exposed nerves, instinctively drawn to anything the least bit soothing to her ego, which had been so badly battered after Wes had abandoned her. Ross's words, his understanding of her need, had acted like a balm to her hurt.

And of course they *were* married. That had been a flimsy way to condone their desire. The truth was, she reminded herself, their marriage was a sham. And now they had made love, which was bound to confuse matters.

Most likely, their desire stemmed from the fact that they had been thrown together under the most intimate circumstances—but that didn't mean a real bond had formed between them. She liked Ross, very much. Who wouldn't like a man who with one sexy look could make her insides melt like butter? But *loved* him? Despite Ross's caring attitude toward her and the wonderful things he'd done to her on that rug, she was certain he wasn't in love with her. In fact, he probably would have ten times rather have gone to Switzerland on business than honeymooned here with her.

Only now perhaps he thought her compliance of last night meant that she would want to continue their little fling. Or that they could go on playing house indefinitely.

She had made a dreadful, dreadful mistake.

Her mind whirred fuzzily, attempting to generate

routes to escape without Ross detecting that she was awake. She had an exit door scoped out. The tough decision was whether she should try to throw on her clothes quickly and run for the door, or snatch her clothes and streak for it. Visualizing running into one of the servants during her dash, plan A seemed the better option.

She grabbed what was in reach—her blouse and skirt and one shoe. She quickly put the blouse on, but slipping on the skirt was going to be more of a challenge, what with Ross's hand braced over her leg. She decided she might just have to make a clean fast break for the door, servants be damned.

She turned and raised herself up on one heel, like a sprinter readying herself for the start of a hundred-yard dash. But just as she was about to rocket for the door, that hand on her leg clamped down hard, preventing movement.

She gasped, turned and saw Ross staring up at her. His grin mirrored the bear's.

"Leaving so soon?"

She combed her fingers nervously through her limp-feeling hair. "Soon? We've been on this floor all night."

He laughed. "I know. I feel like a pretzel."

He was the best-looking pretzel she'd ever seen. She wouldn't have thought it possible, but his bronzed skin was even more magnificent in broad daylight than by the glow of the fire. He was absolutely gorgeous; just gawking at him made her secretly wish he would reach up and pull her down to him again.

"I'm a little, uh, bent out of shape myself. I was just going to take a shower."

"Mind if I join you?"

"Yes! I mean..." She meant *yes.* She would mind. Every single atom of her being minded. Never had she had a shower with a man before. That seemed more intimate somehow than all their delicious acts of the night before put together.

His eyes glinted at her in the morning light. "We could pretend we were standing under a waterfall in that Hawaiian paradise you used to dream about."

Maybe she shouldn't have told him that silly idea she'd always harbored about a tropical honeymoon getaway. It was so silly. And yet his mentioning it to her now made her feel a notch closer to being in love with him than she was before he'd awakened.

He remembered...

And that seemed about as dangerous as sleeping with a real grizzly bear would have been. The last time she'd fallen in love, things hadn't worked out too well.

"Listen, Ross. I know we got carried away last night...."

He sat up and cupped a hand at the back of her head and pressed his lips to her cheek. Alison froze, trying to think of each sensation zipping through her in clinical terms. Her excitement was merely a reaction to skin touching skin, which made nerves relay snappily all the way to her brain, which in turn sent a message to her toes to curl. Emotion really had very little to do with anything.

"As I was saying," she continued, her voice sounding a tad less forceful even to her own ears, "I know we got carried away last night, but that's no reason things between us need change."

One of his eyebrows quirked upward. "It isn't?"

She shook her head. "Do you think?"

Obviously he did. He looked at her doubtfully.

It was just as she suspected. He naturally assumed that after last night she was his for the asking. That they were now somehow inevitably drawn into a romantic entanglement, which would probably suit him just fine for a few months. Then, after an appropriate amount of time for his father's sake, which coincidentally would probably be the same amount of time it took Ross to tire of being saddled with a permanent relationship, she would be shuttled off to Mexico for her divorce, and that would be the end of that. Except that she would end up feeling raw and wounded again and once more would have to resort to cookies and convent retreats to get over him.

Better to get rid of him now than get over him later.

Alison took a deep breath. ''We should cut this honeymoon short.''

He blinked. ''That's some 'good morning.'''

''It's not that last night wasn't...wonderful, but I just think we were reacting to the atmosphere and to the fact that we were married. We weren't thinking clearly.''

He rubbed his jaw pensively. ''Now that you mention it,'' he continued, ''you're right. I wasn't using my head.''

For some perverse reason, his words stung. ''Are you saying that you think our making love was a mistake?'' She quickly added, ''Like I do?''

His lips moved into a half smile. ''Not at all. I'm just saying that for once in my life, I acted with my heart. Something in me responded to you, and I didn't stop to think it through.''

He had a crazy way of saying something that bumped her up, then in the next second something else that bumped her back down again. ''You pitied me,'' she said. That was what she got for yammering on about honeymoons and Wes's dumping her.

"No, it wasn't pity." He shrugged. "I'm not sure what it was. But I suppose you're right. Acting from the heart is rather foolish, isn't it?"

She swallowed and forced her head to bob up and down in a stiff nod. Having a man talk to her about his vulnerable heart was a little too seductive to be safe. Besides, he was changing his mind awfully quickly. She'd either been very persuasive or his heart didn't hold much sway in his life.

"And we have been in close proximity for a few days," Ross went on, making her want to give him a solid slap. "That was bound to influence us."

She gritted her teeth. "That's just what I meant."

He stared at her long and hard, with such intensity in those blue eyes that she felt as if she might melt into the floor. "There's just one thing that bothers me about cutting our honeymoon short," he said.

She nodded. "I know what you mean." Once the honeymoon was over, so, in effect, was their marriage. Oh, sure, they would remain legally bound to each other for a few more months. But they wouldn't really have any contact. Why would they? Ross had his hotel empire, she had her business. He would go to Switzerland, she would return to Dallas. They might exchange a few phone calls, tops.

Although she wasn't in love with Ross, she had grown to care about him. They were friends, as intimate as friends could become in a matter of days.

"It's going to be awfully hard to explain to Dad," he finished.

She gaped at him. Here she was going all mushy and sentimental, thinking about their *friendship,* and all he was considering was whether or not they would be able to keep his father believing the lie. ‘‘I’m sure we can think of something.’’

He wrinkled his brow. ‘‘When would you like to leave?’’

The answer to that question didn’t take much thought. ‘‘As soon as possible.’’

A DEAL WAS A DEAL. He’d always lived by that motto.

So why was he having such a hard time accepting it now?

Ross put the jet’s cell phone back in its cradle and turned to Alison. Her eyes were glued to the window and her hands were clutching the arms of her seat in a white-knuckled grasp. She really didn’t like these little planes.

If things hadn’t been so tense between them, he would have sat down next to her, put his arm around her shoulder, kissed her and told her that everything seemed perfectly normal. They hadn’t even hit any real turbulence to speak of. But he had the distinct feeling that touching her now would only make things worse.

‘‘I’ve arranged to go to Switzerland day after tomorrow,’’ he informed her.

She peeled her gaze away from the window long enough to send him a weak smile.

‘‘I leave from Dallas,’’ he said.

She nodded.

He frowned. No invitation to stay at her apartment ensued—not even a ‘‘Let’s have lunch.’’

Why was it so hard for him to accept the cold truth? Alison just wasn’t interested in him. Or wasn’t interested in him long-term, that is. He wasn’t sure why—

maybe she was still too damaged after Wes. Maybe she was a little too much like Cara after all—career-minded. Or maybe she just didn't think she could love him. No matter the cause, no amount of hinting at a future relationship seemed to capture her fancy.

Given the way she reacted to a simple kiss on the cheek this morning, he hadn't been able to bring himself to tell her the true extent of his feelings. Would she have believed him, anyway, if he'd told her that he'd dreamed all night of them falling in love, of never getting a divorce? Probably not. She didn't seem to trust him, although she had been trusting and womanly soft and more giving than he'd ever known a woman to be last night.

Last night… In his experience, lovemaking like that didn't happen every day. Or even once in a decade. Was Alison so wary of men that she was willing to throw such a wonderful thing away with both hands?

Apparently she was. And he wasn't so certain of his own feelings, either. Was he just being carried away by their circumstances, as Alison suggested, or was he really falling in love?

"We can tell your father that we cut the trip short because you had important business in Switzerland," she said in clipped tones.

He nodded. "I think that will work."

She sighed, then stared out the window again.

"There *is* one thing I think we need to discuss, though," he said.

She glanced at him curiously. "What?"

"Felicity."

She paled. "What about her?"

"Well, I'd always assumed that when we…divorced I would simply tell Dad that you had been granted custody of Felicity. And maybe we could say that you moved across the country or something.''

''That sounds fine.''

''But it's not,'' Ross told her. ''You played your role too well, and now Dad thinks you're this wonderful person. You would never keep Felicity away from him.''

''Of course not!'' She frowned, confused. ''But I've got to. I mean, *I* won't have Felicity.''

''Right.''

''Oh, dear,'' she said, drawn into the muddle. ''Well, I suppose we could ask Sister Joan if we could borrow Felicity from time to time.''

''You mean, rent her?'' Ross asked, smiling ruefully. A few days ago she had thought him repugnant for wanting to use the child in that manner.

''We have a relationship with Felicity now,'' she said defensively. ''It would hardly be *renting*. Felicity loves us. We're the only parents she knows.''

He stared at her evenly. ''But what if someone else adopts her?''

''Oh, no!'' Alison cried with more vehemence than he would have expected from her.

''Don't you want her to have a home?''

Alison frowned. ''Of course I do. But who is going to adopt her? How will we know they're good people?''

''Sister Joan will make sure of that.''

Alison laughed humorlessly. ''That lady would sell her mother superior if it would help out the convent. Any rich couple could waltz in and take Felicity—and you know that doesn't necessarily mean she'll have a good life.''

He sat down next to her. He shared her sentiments

completely, but what could they do? "She's not ours, Alison."

"I know, I know," she said. "But if we could just think of something. Maybe we could make it so that we adopted her secretly and she lived out at the ranch with your father and Hannah. She loves Henry."

He shook his head. "Dad's old. Felicity seems like a handful now, but in a few months, like the man said, you ain't seen nothing yet. She's going to be a hell-raiser extraordinaire."

Alison grumbled her agreement. "But…"

His heart went out to her. He'd grown attached to Felicity, too. And to Alison. In fact, for all her arguments against his original plan to bring his father a grandchild, Alison had never hit on the one that seemed to be his downfall: *What if the lie really worked?* He'd never guessed he would become so emotionally involved with his facade life. Four days ago he was just a businessman. Now he had a whole shadow life he was attached to more than he was to any hotel.

And yet he was going to be forced to give them up. And soon. He looked regretfully down at Alison. She still had that white-knuckled grip on the seat, but she wasn't staring out the window. She didn't even seem aware that they were flying—which made him think that there must be another reason entirely for the panicky look in her eye.

"We have to tell him the truth," she said. She looked as though she'd rather eat nails.

He nodded. "That's what I was going to suggest."

She glanced up at him. "We'll look like fools."

He nodded again. "If the shoe fits…"

"I guess it will be a relief to have it all over." She

laughed, then sighed. ''Obviously I wasn't cut out for marriage.''

Ross couldn't tell how much she was joking. "I think you were,'' he said in a gravelly voice he hadn't expected.

Her eyes widened, then she looked quickly away, her grip still strangling the arm of her chair.

THE GANG WAS all there—Henry and Babs, Sister Joan and her cohorts. Everyone expressed astonishment that Alison and Ross had to come back so early, despite Ross's protests that business, unfortunately, had to come before pleasure. Alison assured everyone, probably about fifty times too often, that she certainly didn't want to stand between Ross and his work.

She couldn't wait to tell Henry the truth so they could end this charade.

The minute they arrived at the house she bounded upstairs to see Felicity, who was fast asleep. Next to her crib, Hannah had left a radio tuned to an oldies station playing at low volume. Alison smiled. Still worked like a charm.

Sister Joan came in on her heels and shut the door behind them. ''All right, what's wrong?'' she asked, peering at Alison knowingly.

''Nothing,'' Alison said, but knew she sounded far from convincing.

''Yes, there is. Why did you cut the honeymoon short? I thought you two were trying to convince everyone you're really a couple.''

Alison sighed in resignation. No sense trying to lie to Sister Joan. ''We were, but we decided it would be for the best if we told Henry and Mother the truth.''

The nun scowled and planted her fists on her hips. "Best for whom, might I ask?"

Alison was taken aback. She thought Sister Joan would *approve* of their confessing. "Best for Henry, Mother, us, Felicity...everybody!"

Sister Joan practically hopped on her toes in agitation. "Do you know what I've accomplished these last two days?"

Alison shook her head.

"Not one, but *two* billiard tables for the youth recreation center. A hundred extra square feet in the nursery—more play room. Your father-in-law even promised to have his architect draw up plans for a gymnasium."

"What are you running over there—a health club?" Alison frowned. "Besides, he's not my father-in-law. Not really. Don't you see? We've got to tell them the truth. Even if we went through a divorce, we still wouldn't have a way to explain why he couldn't see Felicity anymore."

Sister Joan didn't miss a beat. "Tell him you took custody and moved out of state."

"What if he wanted to come visit—or wanted to send a plane ticket for Felicity to visit him?" She shook her head. "It wouldn't work."

"You can't expect us to give up all our projects," Sister Joan said. "Not just because you don't have the ingenuity to figure out a few little pitfalls."

"Not *little* pitfalls, Sister Joan—huge gaping ones. I'm sorry about your gym and the rest of it, but we have to tell him the truth. Maybe he won't revoke his donations. Henry's very generous."

Sister Joan looked depressed. "It was all for Felicity."

Alison nodded. "He really loves her." Guilt, guilt, guilt. She wanted to cry.

Sister Joan studied her again for a long moment. Her beady eyes seemed to bore right through Alison's soul. "*You* love her, too. And you love Ross."

She might have made an argument for Felicity, but Alison couldn't accept that she was in love with Ross. "That's absurd. We barely know each other."

"You love him."

"No, I don't!" Alison insisted, knowing her protest sounded too vehement. She took care to speak in more measured tones. "I don't. It's just that we've been through a lot together in a short period of time. But as soon as we can get Henry and Mother alone in a room together, we'll tell them both the truth and that will be that. We'll probably never even see each other again. It's for the best." She looked up at Sister Joan. It was going to be difficult to get a moment alone with her mother and Henry with so many nuns around. "You'll help us get them alone, won't you, Sister?"

Sister Joan sighed regretfully, then patted Alison's knee in understanding. "You know how you can count on me, dear."

IT WAS IMPOSSIBLE to get their parents alone before dinner. The nuns of St. Felicity's had set up an old badminton net in the backyard, and they insisted that everyone join in until it was time for supper. Ten nuns, Henry Templeton and Babs playing badminton. It was quite a spectacle.

Dinner itself, with everyone conversing convivially and treating Alison and Ross like a lovey-dovey new couple, was naturally not the appropriate time to blurt out the truth. Especially not when it seemed that every five minutes another nun was lifting a glass to toast the happiness of the newly enlarged Templeton family.

They really were sweet ladies, Alison thought. She just wished they would button their lips.

After dinner she took Sister Joan aside. ''Don't forget, we need to speak to Mother and Henry alone.''

''Of course, dear, of course. I haven't forgotten,'' Sister Joan assured her in her kindest tone.

Alison felt better as the group repaired to the library—until Sister Lucia proceeded to play Beethoven sonatas on the piano for almost an hour. When she was finished, Sister Mary-Bernadette quickly took her turn with Chopin. That went on for another hour. When Mary-Bernadette's fingers finally gave out on her, Alison looked meaningfully at Sister Joan and hinted, ''You all must be tired. You'll have a long drive back to Dallas tomorrow.''

Sister Joan blinked innocently. ''I couldn't sleep a wink, could you?'' The other nuns shook their heads, almost in unison.

Alison looked at Ross with growing desperation. Their plans were being sabotaged. His eyes told her not to worry. He apparently had a plan of his own.

He yawned. ''Well, I'm bushed,'' he said, stretching. ''Think we'd better hit the hay, sweetie-bunch.''

It took Alison a moment before she realized that *she* was sweetie-bunch. What was he up to? She smiled stiffly. ''Yes, I'm just exhausted.''

They stood up, said their good-nights and repaired to Ross's room upstairs. Hannah had moved Felicity there—along with the all-important radio—and naturally had transferred Alison's things, as well. Alison stared uncomfortably at her suitcase where it lay sprawled across Ross's king-size bed.

"What have you got up your sleeve?" she asked him after he'd come in behind her and shut the door quietly.

He smiled. "We were never going to outlast those nuns. Especially not if they kept playing that snooze music on the piano."

Alison laughed. "But how are we going to get our parents up here to talk to them?"

"The sisters will probably let them go to bed now that we're gone. And as Dad and your mom come up the stairs, we'll snag them and make our confession."

They had no time to dwell on what they were going to have to tell their folks, however. They could hear footsteps coming down the hall. "That's probably your dad," Alison said. Henry had the next-closest room.

Ross was halfway to the door when there came the unmistakable sound of a key turning the tumblers. As if someone was locking them in!

Alison jumped to her feet and ran to the door, shaking it. Sure enough, the knob wouldn't budge. "That wily Sister Joan!" she cried. She looked at Ross. "This is ridiculous. Don't you have a key?"

He stared at her in dismay. "No, I've never needed one."

She put her hands on her hips. "They can't do this—they can't." She banged on the door and was about to yell for someone to let them out when Ross grabbed her fist.

He nodded toward Felicity, who had awakened and was fussing in her crib. "But what can we do?" she asked Ross as she crossed the room and picked Felicity up. She smelled baby sweet. Alison had missed that smell. And also the way her soft hair felt to the touch.

Don't bond, she reminded herself.

Too late, her heart answered.

"I'll just call down to the kitchen line and tell Hannah to come rescue us," Ross said, going over to the phone.

Alison was amazed that Felicity calmed down so quickly. "Look, Ross—I didn't even have to sing to her." All she'd done was pick her up, cradle her on her shoulder and rub her back gently. Felicity seemed as happy as a kitten.

Ross watched in wonder for a moment, then put the phone receiver to his ear. His eyes widened in dismay. "There's no dial tone," he said, looking down.

Alison went over to inspect. Someone had removed the wire that plugged into the wall from the phone. "Those tricky devils!"

Ross shook his head. "Well, short of raising a ruckus, I don't see what we can do."

Alison glanced down at Felicity's gentle breathing. Then she looked at the windows. "Could we climb down?"

"There's a flagstone border all around this side of the house. If we fell, we'd break our necks."

She wasn't that desperate. Yet.

She glanced anxiously at the bed, then at Ross. "I hate to admit defeat, but..."

He nodded. "We can tell them tomorrow," he quickly agreed. "Another twelve hours won't matter."

It wouldn't to their parents, Alison amended. But she and Ross would have to sleep together again. Which is precisely what she'd wanted to avoid.

He looked at her knowingly. "I understand what

you're worried about. But I guarantee, nothing will happen."

She hadn't expected anything to happen last night, either. But then, without exchanging so much as a "Would you care to..." they had spent the night in carnal oblivion on a bearskin rug. Who knew what could happen in a bed!

She looked around the room and spotted a settee in the corner. She nodded to it. "I can sleep there."

Ross didn't like the idea. "I couldn't let you do that," he said. "That thing's bound to be uncomfortable. Besides, you're a guest here."

"Well, you can't fit on it," she told him, a glance up and down his six-foot-plus frame affirming the validity of that statement.

"If you sleep on the settee," he said, "I'll sleep on the floor."

"But that makes no sense!" she protested.

"It makes no sense for either of us to be uncomfortable when there's a huge soft bed just waiting there. Believe me, it's so big you won't even know I'm there."

Yeah, right. Alison glanced at him skeptically. There was no way she would *not* know that Ross was lying just inches away from her. She wouldn't sleep a wink.

But if sleeping on the settee meant neither of them was going to sleep a wink, then what was the point of arguing?

"Okay," she said, giving in reluctantly. Ross was surely right. They were both so regretful after the night before nothing would happen.

It would simply be their last night together as husband and wife. Nothing more to it than that.

Chapter Eleven

Ross awoke with a peculiar feeling. At first he wasn't certain why everything seemed so disconcerting. He was sleeping in his bedroom in the home that had been his home and then his home away from home for as long as he could remember. The air smelled sweet, of baby shampoo, which reminded him that they had awakened in the night to feed Felicity with the bottle that someone had kindly put inside their door while they were sleeping. He opened his eyes and saw the baby lying on her back, deep in infant dreamland. Facing him was Alison, looking perfectly beautiful in sleep. Their bodies formed a warm human cradle for Felicity.

Everything seemed fine—blissful, almost.

Then he figured out what was wrong.

Nothing.

For the first time in a long time, he hadn't awakened from sleep consumed with worry over business or something else that needed to be done or his father. He didn't have a plan in his head. He was just content.

He felt complete—as if all his father's admonitions lo these many years had been true. Here he was with a family of his own, and life had never seemed so good, so whole. Okay, so maybe they were just rented for the weekend, but the result was the same. And he liked the feeling.

He liked *them.* Loved them. It was a revelation.

And just when he was really getting the swing of being a husband and father, his tenure as both was up. There would be no more playing with Felicity after today, no more singing to her with Alison. How could you just give up a baby you'd come to think of as your own?

And Alison. How could he let her go? He would miss sparring with her. And joking with her. And the way her mouth quirked into a reluctant smile sometimes when she just couldn't make herself stay angry. When he was with her, it felt as if he was living for that smile, that indication she liked him, no matter how hard she had tried not to. And he would miss holding her in his arms, kissing her, making love to her. Their physical union had seemed so right, so perfect.

The three of them seemed perfect together. And yet they had been brought together through completely artificial means, with no thought given to compatibility. He might have picked any baby in Dallas to take to his father, but he hadn't. He'd chosen Felicity, and now, after less than a week, he felt irretrievably attached to her. He'd found Alison, and now he couldn't contemplate the idea of relinquishing her to her old life.

The laws of statistics, learned so long ago in a cold classroom in New Haven, swam through his mind. But he realized suddenly that trying to reason out love was nonsense. Sometimes a gambler rolling for double sixes hit it lucky—which apparently was what he had done.

And now his luck seemed to be at an end.

How many moments in their lives would he miss? How many times in the months and maybe years ahead would something happen to him that would make him wonder what Alison would have thought, or how different something would have seemed if she had been there to share it with him? He felt foolish for thinking it, and yet he couldn't help wishing he could have them here at the ranch for Christmas. And what about Felicity's first birthday? How could he allow that to go by without having Felicity there to shower with little dresses and stuffed animals and books that he could read aloud to her at bedtime and on long rainy Saturday afternoons?

How could he let them go?

A few weeks back Ross would have said that after people got married, everything went downhill. He would have pointed out the inevitable monotony of living with the same woman for fifty or so years, the sure-to-happen quarrels that could make life so trying, the terrible tedium of dealing with in-laws and your wife's friends and most of all, children. Marriage was a trap, a snare, an unwanted distraction from the far more fascinating business of running a hotel empire.

Funny that now, looking at Alison and Felicity, so peaceful in sleep, monotony was the furthest thing from his mind. All he could imagine were warm firelit nights, romantic whirlwind vacations—with a baby!—and the endless occupation of discovering every facet of another person for, say, fifty or so years. Years of tedium now seemed more like years of bliss.

Before he could give the matter another thought, he reached over and gently nudged Alison's shoulder. "Alison—wake up."

She shrugged and let out a little grunt of dismay.

"Hey, sleepyhead," he said, nudging her again, "wake up. We have to talk."

She wrinkled her nose, testing the air, and slowly allowed one eyelid to squint open. She saw him and her nose wrinkled again. "Talk about what?" she mumbled sleepily.

"About us."

"Oh." She flopped over so that her back was to him.

He chuckled, and kept his hand gently on her shoulder. "I think we should stay married."

Her head bobbed. "Okay."

He frowned. Had she heard him correctly?

Just as he was about to ask, Alison shot up and turned to him. "Did I hear you right?"

He nodded. "I don't think we should get a divorce."

She looked at him as though he were as crazy as a bedbug—and as desirable to be near. "That's insane!"

"Not really." He felt reckless, like that gambler rolling for doubles.

Her expression turned suspicious. "You mean that we should stay married for longer than we had planned? A few more months, maybe?"

"No, I mean forever."

Her jaw dropped. "But that's impossible."

"Why?" He leaned forward farther and said excitedly, "We're neither of us attached to anyone. We could provide a home for Felicity and companionship for each other. Haven't you sort of enjoyed these past few days?"

Alison smirked. "Oh, I get it. And while we're in

the family-acquiring mood, why not adopt another child or two?''

He nodded enthusiastically. ''Or even have one or two of our own.''

She stopped smiling. ''This must be some kind of joke, right?''

''Why would you think that?''

''Because you don't just marry someone because you *sort of enjoy* their company, Ross. Or because you happen to be unattached and you decide it would be a good time to take on a spouse and child.''

''Why not?''

She tossed her hands up in the air. ''Because you just don't, that's all.''

''A couple of days ago you told me that people just didn't rent children or marry to spare a parent's feelings, but I did, and what's more, I've found I like it. So why put an end to a situation that's working perfectly well and to the benefit of all of us?''

She tilted her head skeptically. ''Wait a second. I can see where you might benefit from having a ready-made family, and I can really see that Felicity benefits, but I don't see where I stand to benefit here.''

He blinked. ''You don't?''

''No!'' she cried in exasperation. ''Ross, I don't know if you realize this, but I was doing just fine before I met you.''

''I thought you were such a mess you ended up at a convent retreat to recuperate.''

She shrugged and admitted, ''Okay, so things weren't *perfect.* But they weren't so desperate that I was ready to jump into a marriage with a man I barely knew.''

''But that's exactly what you did do.''

"I know! But not because I really wanted to. Ross, do you realize how little we know each other? I don't know what your favorite color is or what political party you vote for or even where you live."

"Green, Independent, Houston," he replied. "There. Now you know."

"It's not that easy," she said. "For one thing, there's Houston. My business is in Dallas. What am I supposed to do—just close up shop?"

He frowned. "I wouldn't want you to do that...."

"Should I commute to Houston, then?"

"I could commute," he said. "Or really, there's no reason why the office has to be in Houston. It's just always been there."

"It's easy to say these things now, Ross, but once we started dealing with the reality of negotiating what I want and what you want, things would start getting a lot dicier."

"How do you know?"

"I just know," she said. "Even when I was getting ready to move in with Wes, we would fight over details. It took us forever just to decide what couch we wanted to buy. That issue alone almost made us call off the engagement."

Ross stared stonelike at her. She obviously didn't care much for him at all if she wasn't even willing to consider the idea of staying with him.

He took a moment to nurse his wounded pride. He'd never thought that the woman he finally proposed marriage to would consider the possibility so unthinkable. Especially when she was married to him already.

Looking as if she felt as awkward as he did, Alison got off the bed and padded to her suitcase. She opened it and took out jeans and a shirt, saying, "You just have to think of this as you do a vacation. A vacation can be fun, or a nightmare or a mixture of both, but it doesn't have anything to do with the reality of day-to-day living."

He nodded, although he wasn't convinced, and he was beginning to wonder if she was, either. She skittered around the room, throwing on her clothes and brushing her hair, then escaped into the bathroom. "Once we get back to our normal lives, our heads will be clearer."

Our heads, she'd said. Ross smiled. She wasn't quite as detached as she pretended to be.

"You think so?" he called out to her, leaning back in bed. Felicity blinked up at him sleepily, then began wiggling her arms and legs fitfully. He tickled her tummy, bringing forth a burst of giggles.

"Absolutely," Alison told him from behind the closed door. "Once I'm in Dallas and you're in Switzerland or Houston or wherever, this will all seem very far away."

His grin widened as a plan formed in his head. She sounded as if she *hoped* it would all seem far away. Maybe he would just have to *make* it all unforgettable. "I suppose you're right. But if it's all the same to you, I would rather wait a few days before we tell the folks the truth. Everything's happened so fast. I'm still a little worried about Dad's health, you know."

There was a pause. "Well...okay," she said reluctantly. "But we shouldn't wait too long."

"No, we won't." Which meant there would be no time to waste. He bent down and nuzzled Felicity's little upturned nose with his own. "What do you think about us trying to get you a permanent mommy?" he asked her in a low whisper.

She rewarded him with an impatient baby-fist sock to the jaw.

Ross laughed. "Okay, okay," he told Felicity. "I'll get to work on it right away."

THE DOOR TO HER OFFICE opened and Dee took a few steps inside. At least, Alison assumed the legs and platform shoes peeping out from beneath the huge bouquet belonged to her assistant. The rest of Dee was completely hidden by flowers.

Alison jumped up from her desk and inspected this latest delivery. She knew the huge arrangement of tropical flowers were from Ross—she'd received something from him every day since she'd returned to Dallas—but she still wanted to find out for sure. She picked the small envelope off one of the ribbons and read the message inside.

Did you remember our one-week anniversary?

Alison sighed. One week ago yesterday—she hadn't forgotten. She'd sat by the phone in the apartment, half expecting Ross to call. But he hadn't.

Dee's brow poked up inquisitively. "From Ross?"

Alison took the flowers from her, making a show of rolling her eyes and huffing in exasperation. But she carefully placed the gorgeous arrangement next to her Don Ho CD, her basket of coconuts and champagne, and the tiny miniature Jaguar car she hadn't stopped fiddling with since the day Ross had sent it to her.

Dee sighed. "I wish some cute guy showered me with stuff every day."

Alison put her hands on her hips, trying to tamp down that giddy reaction Ross's presents always seemed to give her. She wasn't sure what he was up to. Did he feel guilty? Want to pursue a relationship with her? Why didn't he just call?

"You'd feel differently if the cute guy was your husband," she said acerbically, trying to disguise her frayed nerves.

"That's the best part of all," Dee said. "He's obviously crazy about you."

"Or just plain crazy," Alison pointed out. "Before we left the ranch, I told him I wanted to get a divorce."

"Maybe he doesn't want you to."

"But he agreed with me," Alison said, confused by Ross's puzzling long-distance behavior. It was almost as if he was trying to woo her special delivery. "We hashed it all out."

"He didn't say anything about wanting to stay married?" Dee probed.

"Yes—he argued the case for staying married for all of five minutes."

"But you convinced him you should get a divorce."

Alison cross her arms. "The man didn't take much convincing."

Dee shook her head. "I still say, if a man marries you, even spontaneously, it must mean something. Don't you ever watch Oprah? Most men take years to drag to the altar, even when they're really in love. You just got lucky, girl, and snagged one off-the-cuff."

Alison glanced anxiously at all the presents Ross had sent her since her return. She knew he was in Switzerland, but his gifts loomed in her office to remind her of their short history together. It was tempting to think he loved her, but she knew better. If he did, he'd had ample opportunity to tell her so, and his failure to do so could only mean he was angling for an affair with his "wife."

Why wouldn't he accept the inevitable and leave her alone?

"He married me for convenience," she said, trying to put aside thoughts of loneliness that had been tormenting her since her return from the Templeton ranch. "The same way he rented Felicity. Then he decided that a wife would be a nice thing to have around the house, I guess."

Dee's eyes narrowed in speculation. "I wonder what made him think that?"

Alison blushed, remembering their night on the bearskin rug. "Never mind. The point is, the man has never considered anything so pertinent as *love.* In all his arguments for staying married, he never even mentioned that he liked me, much less loved me. Can you imagine? He just told me it was nice to have companionship."

"Well, isn't it?" Dee asked.

"Of course! But if you're talking marriage, as in 'happily ever after,' there has to be more to the equation. Take Wes and me, for example. We were in love, and then it still didn't work out."

Dee frowned dubiously, but didn't say anything.

Alison tilted her head. "What?" she asked, trying to squeeze Dee's thoughts out of her. "Are you saying Wes and I *weren't* in love?"

"Let me put it this way," Dee said. "Do you wish you were married to Wes?"

"Of course not!" Alison was amazed Dee would even ask such a thing. "After what that creep did to me?"

Dee shrugged. "Oh, but don't all men do creepy

things from time to time? Take this Ross guy, for instance..."

Even hearing the two men compared made the blood rush to Alison's cheeks. "Ross is nothing like Wes," she declared vehemently. "He might be a little strong-willed and persistent—and, all right, maybe even a little arrogant—but he's not a *creep*. Even all the shady things he did, like renting a baby and marrying me, he did because he loved his dad. If anything, his big fault is caring too much about other people. Like with Felicity, he..."

Her words faded away in the face of Dee's complacent grin. "And you're *sure* you're not in love with this guy?"

Alison hugged her arms and shuffled her feet. "Of course not."

Dee nodded. "Uh-huh, I see. Just sticking up for the hubby."

Alison said nothing.

"Oh, by the way—" Dee changed to a more businesslike tone "—the photographer called about the head shots he took the other day. John said he's sending the contact sheets over."

Alison nodded and went back to her desk. After Dee left, however, she gave up trying to look busy, rested her chin on one hand and rolled the little Jaguar across her desk pad.

She needed to stop thinking about Ross. But how could she when he sent her these presents every day?

The trouble was, she didn't have enough to occupy her mind. Work seemed routine, and when she was back in her apartment, she felt like climbing the walls. There was nothing to do but watch TV, which suddenly seemed to consist of family sitcoms, police dramas and made-for-TV-movies with situations that didn't seem half as compelling as the one she found herself in. Married, but not married. Bonded with a child she had no relation to, no right to love. And yet she did love Felicity. She missed her.

Where was Sister Joan when she needed her? The cagey old nun had abandoned her just when she would have enjoyed seeing her. Alison had taken to visiting the nursery at St. Felicity's after work, but it just wasn't the same as being around Felicity all the time. Felicity was usually taking a nap, and Alison didn't feel she had the right to wake her just to play. And she didn't think the nuns would look too kindly on her asking to borrow Felicity for an evening.

It wasn't fair to Felicity, anyway.

She began to gather up her things, steeling herself for another restless night in her apartment. As she hoisted her purse over her shoulder, she twisted her prop wedding ring, which for some foolish reason she still wore. She just had to find a hobby or take up bridge—anything to get her mind off the husband and baby that weren't hers.

HENRY AND BABS sat in companionable silence, munching air-popped popcorn as they watched an old Doris Day musical on the afternoon movie of the local television station. It had become their routine during the week and a half Babs had been staying at the ranch. Babs wasn't in any hurry to leave her luxurious surroundings, and Henry, who was a little lonely for Ross and Felicity, wasn't in any hurry to have her go.

"You know, some people said I was the spitting image of Doris back in my younger years," Babs said during a commercial.

"In your Day, you might say," Henry quipped, laughing. Then he frowned, thinking. "I wonder if that means Felicity will grow up to resemble Doris Day."

Babs looked doubtful. "I've come to the opinion that the child is the spitting image of Ross. And Ross looks nothing like Doris Day, thank heavens."

"He never could sing worth a darn, either," Henry added for good measure. "Did you hear him on the phone the other night? Nearly wore my ear out. Don't know how Felicity can stand it."

"Maybe she'll also inherit her father's tin ear."

Henry beamed that proud-grandpa grin at her, then frowned again. "But you know, I thought she kind of resembled Alison myself." He bumped his fist impatiently against the upholstered arm of the couch. "I wish that girl of yours would call."

His guest made a *tsk*ing noise. "You know, Henry, I'm ashamed to say this, but my daughter is not very good at keeping up with people. In fact, if you hadn't called me the morning of the wedding, I, her own mother, might never have found out about the marriage or Ross or even Felicity."

Henry gaped at her. "Alison never told you about Felicity?"

Babs wrung her hands in remembered wounded maternal pride. "Well, how *was* I to know? She wouldn't see me for a year. We had a...falling-out. And Alison is always so busy with her work."

Henry shook his head. "That's a terrible thing. Me, I always like things to be open and honest between parent and child. Of course, Ross didn't tell me about Alison and Felicity, either...."

They stood staring blankly at the diaper commercial on the television, Henry reflecting on the ups and downs of being a parent, Babs wishing that they could have a little more salt on the popcorn. Of course, since sodium was bad for Henry's hypertension...

Henry smiled and pointed at the screen, where an unhappy baby in a leaky diaper wailed unhappily. "Look there, that little baby looks like Felicity."

Babs broke out in a laugh. "She does! She looks *just* like her. She has the same hair and eyes."

"And little dimple on her cheek," Henry said excitedly, leaning forward. "It's exactly the same, even though the baby's not smiling."

"She has Felicity's cry down, too," Babs noted, as if to imply that this impostor baby must have been studying Felicity's mannerisms on the sly.

"By thunder, I believe that baby *is* Felicity!" Henry announced. He yelled for Hannah. "I bet Hannah would be able to tell for sure. Nothing gets by Hannah."

By the time Hannah came out, however, the crying baby was gone, replaced by a completely different baby in a dry diaper. But the minute she looked at the television, Hannah nodded emphatically. "I know what you're talkin' about. That cryin' baby's the spittin' image of that baby your son says is your grandbaby."

Babs blinked in disbelief, and Henry looked as if he might faint. "The baby Ross *says* is my grandbaby?"

"You mean you think he's lying?" Babs asked, aghast.

Hannah pursed her lips.

"Hannah, what do you know?" Henry demanded.

"Nothin'," Hannah said. "I don't have anything like facts." She paused for dramatic effect and crossed her arms slowly over her ample chest. ''All I got are suspicions.''

Babs and Henry glanced at each other anxiously, then looked back at Hannah as the housekeeper began to weave a strange tale of parents of a six-month-old who still read the instructions on diaper packages, of mysterious arguments behind closed doors, and newlyweds locked into their room at night by nuns. ''And those nuns got me wondering, too,'' Hannah said, looking mighty skeptical. ''Why would a baby be named after a convent? Is your daughter very religious, Mrs. Bennett?''

Babs laughed. ''Alison? Why, she was the terror of her Catholic school!''

Henry stood and began pacing and rubbing his snow-white beard. ''Alison runs a modeling agency, doesn't she?''

Babs nodded. ''A children's modeling agency.'' She snapped her fingers. ''Why, that explains it! She must have signed on her own beautiful child to be one of her clients.''

Henry didn't look convinced. ''And you think two proud parents like Alison and Ross wouldn't have mentioned that their baby had been on television? Heck, they would have brought us a tape!''

Babs deflated somewhat in the face of his undeniably sound argument. ''I suppose you're right.''

Henry continued his inquisition. ''You say you hadn't seen Alison for an entire year before the wedding?''

She nodded, glancing from Henry to Hannah. She wasn't anxious to have her daughter exposed as a liar or be cast out from the Templeton clan. ''She could have been carrying a child in that time,'' she said in

Alison's defense. "Heaven knows, she hasn't managed to lose her pregnancy pudge yet. She might look normal to you, but she used to be rail thin."

Henry discounted the last bit of information and latched onto the former. "But there's a chance she could also *not* have had a child in that time," Henry said. "In fact, there's a very good chance." He picked up the portable phone on the coffee table and began to dial.

"Who are you calling? Alison?" Babs asked anxiously. Her heart beat in terror of the coming humiliation. To think—two failed marriages in a single year! Poor Alison!

Poor Babs!

"No. Ross," Henry corrected, waiting for an answer. His face was red with impatience.

"Oh, Mr. Templeton, watch your blood pressure," Hannah urged.

Henry ignored her, so Babs offered, "Maybe I should call Alison first and feel her out on the subject. There must be a perfectly reasonable explanation."

He shook his head. "Until this matter with Felicity, I've never known my son to lie to me. And now I intend to get a straight answer from Ross himself—do I or do I not have a grandchild?"

THE REAL-ESTATE AGENT flashed a dazzling toothpaste-commercial smile Ross's way. "So, Mr. Templeton, are you married?"

"Good question," he said, inspecting the beautiful old two-story house in front of them. It was perfect—just what he'd been hunting for. Big enough for a family to grow in, but not so large that it wouldn't feel intimate.

He looked back at Jackie, the real-estate agent, who was now smiling in confusion at his vague answer to her simple question. "Yes, I'm married," he finally said.

Her expression turned from flirtatious interest to professional geniality in the bat of an eye. "Any children?"

"Just one—so far."

She chuckled knowingly. "I see," she said. "Apparently you feel you might have a need for all five bedrooms someday."

"We might keep one as a guest room," he joked as they entered the living room. It was large, with light varnished hardwood floors and lined with windows on two sides, giving it an open airy feel. He could just imagine going out with Alison to pick out rugs and chairs and pictures, and then later, in wintertime, cuddling in front of the fireplace that took up one corner of the room.

The blue-and-white-tiled kitchen with its big breakfast nook gave him similarly blissful domestic mental images. Maybe he was being overly optimistic—he hadn't heard from Alison since they'd parted ways at the ranch—but he hoped his plan would be fruitful.

"Does your wife cook?"

"Maybe," he answered absently, looking outside at the big backyard and patio with pool. They would have to put in a swing set soon for Felicity. And, of course, they would have to be careful with that pool....

Jackie kept on smiling, no doubt sensing he was hooked. Given the beauty of the house and its great condition, who wouldn't be sold on it? "Would you like to look at the yard first or shall we go upstairs?"

He hesitated, then his phone, which was clipped to

his belt, chirped loudly at him. Probably a call about Switzerland. The project was in the problem phase that all developments seemed to go through. He glanced apologetically at Jackie. "I'm sorry, would you mind?"

She nodded understandingly and moved a few steps away to give him privacy.

He punched the talk button and put the little digital phone to his ear. "Hello."

"Ross!" his father boomed on the other end of the line. "What the hell is going on with my grandchild— or do I have one?"

Ross felt his stomach lurch. Oh, no! How had his father discovered the truth—or did he actually know it yet? "Have you spoken to Alison?"

"No, I wanted to talk to you first and get some straight answers," Henry said testily. Ross hadn't heard that voice since he'd gotten a D in anthropology. "Are you or are you not married?"

"Of course," Ross said. "You were at the wedding."

His father harrumphed loudly. "I want to know if that wedding was for real. I want to know if you're *really* married."

Ross sensed that the lie was crumbling. Any attempt now to keep it patched together would only make them look more foolish later on when they finally told the truth. He sighed and admitted, "Well, actually, no. I'm not really married."

Jackie's head flicked around, then turned quickly away again. She took a few steps into the next room— but not so far that she wouldn't hear the conversation.

His father said nothing for a long moment. Ross felt like a worm. "Then—"

"I'm sorry, Dad. I don't have a child."

"Then Felicity...?"

"She was just a rental."

His father understood almost immediately. "Ah, I see. You thought I was dying. You thought I would like to see my grandchild—even if she wasn't really mine."

His tone made Ross's actions sound crass to his own ears—much the same as they had sounded to Alison two weeks ago. He had lied to his own father, treating him as if he wasn't a grown-up. All Alison's doomsday predictions proved well-founded.

"Dad, I'm sorry. I don't know what came over me. Suddenly it just seemed the thing to do to have a wife and child. But if it makes you feel any better, the joke turned out to be on me. I'm in love with Alison and Felicity. I really do want a wife and child now. And I plan to get them by hook or by crook."

His father chuckled skeptically, which made Ross feel a little better. Maybe their relationship had not been irreparably damaged by his idiocy. "Well," Henry said, "you seem to have learned a little about the 'by crook' part in your thirty-five years. I'll admit you had me completely bamboozled."

Ross's shoulders sagged. "The only trouble is, I don't want to bamboozle Alison. I want to sweep her off her feet. Unfortunately her feet are pretty firmly grounded, so that's making my job a little harder."

"So your plan is already under way."

Putting a hand on his hip, Ross looked around, inspecting the kitchen for cracks or water damage. There were none. "Yes, with any luck I should be closing up the biggest part of it soon." He looked back out at the patio and pool. "In fact, I've got an invitation for you. And for Babs, too, if she's there."

Henry sounded interested. "An invitation? What for?"

"A luau."

Chapter Twelve

''Another of those faxes just came for you,'' Dee said, dropping a sheet of paper bearing the image of a two-story house onto Alison's desk.

Alison studied the picture with a frown. It was the very same picture someone had been faxing to her office for days now. There was no address attached, no message. It didn't appear to be an advertisement. What could it mean?

''Weird,'' she said, shaking her head. ''Maybe it's some sort of real-estate promotion.'' But she couldn't see what good sending out faxes of houses with no additional information attached would do. Besides, the house, which was gorgeous and homey, nearly offended her professional eye in its bare presentation. ''I wish I could send a message to whomever's been faxing this to us and tell them that the house would look a lot better with a few kids playing in the yard.''

Dee nodded. ''With a couple of golden-retriever puppies.''

A house like that cried out for a family to live in it, Alison thought, feeling an almost painful ache building inside her.

"What's that you're doing?" Dee asked, looking at the sketch on the desk in front of Alison.

Embarrassed, Alison covered the drawing with her forearm and shook her head. She'd been designing a nursery—one that happened to have the same dimensions as the guest bedroom in her apartment. "Oh, I was just doodling," she said, tapping the eraser of her pencil against her desk.

"You're doodling cribs?"

Alison blushed. "Oh…is that what it looks like?"

"Uh-huh," Dee said, reading her like a book. "Have you actually talked to Sister Joan about adopting that baby yet?"

Alison ducked her head. "No, but I intend to. I know they won't want to give a baby to a single mother, but maybe if I prove that I could take good care of her…" She shrugged, knowing she was fighting an uphill battle. "Heck, Rosie O'Donnell did it—and she must be a Catholic, right?"

Dee nodded, looking at her pityingly.

Alison hated that look, but knew she deserved it. She straightened her shoulders and took her hands off her sketch, leaving her nursery-room drawings out in the open for all to see. "Well, why shouldn't I adopt a baby?" she asked. "I have means and a home, and I love Felicity as much as anyone possibly could."

"And you're lonely," Dee finished for her.

Alison nodded, feeling tears well in her eyes. Lonely? There ought to be a new word invented for the deep-down despair and restlessness she felt. Home alone at night, it was as if half of herself had been torn away. She didn't see anything that she didn't want to share with Ross—the husband she had to constantly remind herself she didn't actually have. And a million times a day she worried about Felicity and who was taking care of her, and whether she could remember their time together. And whether she missed her adventure with Alison and Ross.

Alison knew *she* missed her excursion with Felicity and Ross. She missed Ross, period. All those days she had been comparing him to Wes she hadn't been able to see that they were nothing alike. And her feelings for Ross were not at all like those she'd had for Wes. They were much deeper.

She loved Ross as she'd never loved Wes. But she'd been so defensive she'd let him get away from her. From the looks of things, he wasn't coming back. He wasn't even sending flowers anymore.

But there was still Felicity. The two of them, at least, might be able to have each other.

"Call Sister Joan," Dee told her. "Otherwise you're going to torture yourself until you find out whether you have a chance. And even if St. Felicity's turns you down, there are other ways to adopt."

"But I don't want to adopt just *any* baby," Alison said, the idea of rejection panicking her. "I want Felicity."

Dee pushed the phone toward her. "Call."

When Dee left, Alison hesitantly picked up the phone and dialed. When someone answered, Alison asked for Sister Joan.

"Sister Joan isn't here right now. Would you like to speak to Sister Catherine?"

God forbid. Alison remembered her last run-in with the head of St. Felicity's. She doubted Sister Catherine would want to hand over the convent's beloved foundling to someone she considered an unrepentant berry-bush killer. "No, thank you—I'll call back later."

She hung up the phone and sighed. Where could Sister Joan be? She never thought she'd see the day she'd want to hunt the woman down, but that was exactly what she found herself wanting to do. Of course, Dallas was a huge city, and Sister Joan could be anywhere, but more than likely she was at one of her favorite haunts—the park near the convent, the local soup kitchen St. Felicity's co-ran with a community group or Whataburger.

Alison did some quick calculations. It was only four in the afternoon, and she was sure there was important work to be done, but what was more important than Felicity? Every moment she let pass was precious time wasted that she could be spending with Felicity. If she'd learned anything in the past year—in the past week—it was that wallowing had gotten her nowhere. If she was going to have the life she wanted, she had to grab for it.

It was time to make that grab.

She hopped up from her desk, tossed on the jacket that had been hanging on the back of her chair and threw her purse over her shoulder. Just as she had taken two purposeful strides toward the door, however, it opened suddenly and Sister Joan barged in, pushing a stroller.

Alison's heart leaped. She ran over and gave the nun a big hug, she was so glad to see her. "Sister Joan, I was just about to go find you!"

Sister Joan chuckled. "Find me? My dear, how did you intend to do that? I'm not predictable—not like you."

The words sounded like a reproach, and Alison knew she deserved them. Wes's deserting her had made her so defensive she doubted she'd done one spontaneous thing in the past year. Until now.

She leaned down to the stroller, clucking her tongue and making silly Felicity noises.

"I should tell you—"

Ignoring Sister Joan's words, Alison pulled the blanket away from Felicity's face—and then drew back with a gasp of surprise.

"This isn't Felicity!"

Sister Joan beamed a proud smile at her. "No, this is a little baby that was left at the convent the other day. Sister Catherine, bless her, is insisting we call her Joan."

Joan! "But where is Felicity?"

Joan's smile disappeared and she avoided the question. "I, uh, thought I would bring Joan in and see what you thought of her."

Alison glanced down distractedly at the baby, who was adorable. But she wasn't Felicity. "Where is Felicity, Sister?"

Sister Joan's shoulders lifted and fell in a heavy sigh. "Well, I hate to tell you this..."

Alison was practically hopping up and down in frustration and just managed to keep herself from shaking the information out of Sister Joan. "Where is she? Is something wrong? What's happened?"

Sister Joan's eyes widened. "Oh, nothing bad has happened."

"Then what?"

"You should be happy." Sister Joan smiled. "Someone has decided to adopt Felicity."

Alison was stunned into silence for a moment. *Someone?* She tried to picture Felicity in someone else's home, crawling around another family's living room. The more she attempted to imagine it, however, the tighter the bands around her chest became. "Who?" she asked finally, the word coming out as a croak.

"Nice people. You'd like them."

Alison fought back the tears in her eyes. "So it's a couple."

Sister Joan nodded, and Alison felt the voice of defeat calling out to her. A couple. That made her, who could only offer Felicity herself and a lot of love, second-best in most people's minds.

Oh, she wished Ross hadn't disappeared! If only she could go to him and tell him that she'd been wrong—that she *did* want to stay a family. That whatever differences they had wouldn't matter as long as they could all be together.

But she didn't even know for sure where Ross was. And now there was the small matter of this nice couple...

Nice. That didn't say much. She knew she didn't have a right to put Sister Joan through an inquisition, but she couldn't help asking, "How do you know they're nice?"

Sister Joan waved the question away as if it hardly mattered. "Oh, you can just tell these things. Good people are good people."

Alison's jaw dropped in astonishment. "Surely you got references from these people, checked them out...?"

The nun nodded. "Naturally. I think we checked them out pretty thoroughly."

"You *think?*" Alison practically shrieked. "I'd imagine you'd be a little more concerned for Felicity's welfare, after all she's done for St. Felicity's!"

"They're very wealthy, Alison."

"That doesn't mean they'll make good parents."

"Of course not—although you have to admit it helps." Sister Joan's forehead became lined with worry. "Actually it's the couple that's concerned. You see, they're a little suspicious of Felicity, because she's so temperamental and all."

Alison nearly exploded. "But she's not temperamental—not when she's around people she loves and who love her and take the time to sing to her and play with her." She took a few deep breaths to keep herself from blowing a gasket. "Who are these people to go around asking questions about Felicity, when *they're* the ones who should be checked out for temperament flaws!"

Sister Joan tried to soothe Alison's ruffled feathers. "Now, now. I'm glad you've taken such an interest in the Van Hoffelmeyer-Burnsteads."

Hearing the name, Alison's dislike for the "nice" couple rose another notch. *Van Hoffelmeyer-Burnsteads!* Probably the pair was a joining of two such socially prominent families that they couldn't bear not to trumpet their complete pedigree to the world. "I only want to know that they'll be good parents," she said defensively.

"Fine. You can find out for yourself."

Alison eyed the nun suspiciously. "How?"

"They want to talk to you."

"To me?" Alison squeaked.

"Yes, you know—to vouch for Felicity's character." Sister Joan smiled. "I told them that *you* were just wild about Felicity."

Alison didn't think she could take any more. "If these people don't like Felicity, why don't they go find themselves another baby?'' She looked down at little Joan. ''Why don't you give them this one? She looks like she'd be happy being a Van Hooplewinkle-Barnside.''

''Van Hoffelmeyer-Burnstead,'' Sister Joan corrected sternly. ''They want Felicity because she's so cute—and she was on that commercial.''

''Oh, honestly!'' Alison cried in disgust.

''Now I don't want you to go see these people if you aren't going to be civil,'' Sister Joan said. ''They're really being very bighearted taking Felicity. She's getting older, you know, and most couples want newborns.''

Alison crossed her arms and scowled. Civil? She would like to wring their long aristocratic necks. Some rich couple who decided they had a kind of noblesse oblige to adopt a foundling they'd seen on TV—as long as she was quiet and housebroken.

Sister Joan continued, ''I think your putting in a word for Felicity would make all the difference to their decision.''

Suddenly Alison's ears perked up. ''You mean they're really sitting on the fence?''

''Unfortunately yes. But I believe they *will* adopt Felicity—especially after you assure them what a sweetheart she is.''

Alison froze, praying silently that the thoughts running through her mind couldn't be seen in her expression. Because they were devilish thoughts, selfish thoughts. Although...wouldn't she be acting in Felicity's interest? Felicity was too strong-willed and high-spirited to be happy in a stiff snobbish family.

Felicity as a debutante?

Never!

Alison forced a smile. "Of course I'll go see the Van Hoffelmeyer-Whosits. It was selfish of me not to volunteer earlier."

"Burnsteads." Sister Joan tilted her head. "Why selfish? Were *you* thinking of adopting Felicity?"

Alison hesitated. She didn't want to blow it. Especially not when she had rivals. Once she'd annihilated the competition—and it sounded as if that job wouldn't be too difficult—she would make her case to Sister Joan. "Oh, I was toying with the idea, maybe. But it was just a whim, I'm sure."

"I should hope so," Sister Joan said. "We really want our baby to go to a couple, you know."

A *nice* couple, Alison thought, her teeth on edge. She nodded and smiled, nodded and smiled.

"Now, I brought their address with me..." Sister Joan said, rooting through her purse.

She handed Alison a slip of paper with the address of the Van Hoffelmeyer-Burnsteads' house. Of course their home was in Highland Park, the oldest and toniest section of town. She bet the place was gorgeous. Picture-perfect.

"I thought you could pay them a visit after we spoke about little Joan," Sister Joan said, distracted by her latest protégée. "I think you'll find she's a perfectly proportioned child—and *very* photogenic. Like that baby in those tire ads..."

"HERE'S THE TAPE you wanted," Dee said. "Although I don't know what purpose a bunch of outtakes from some old commercial could possibly have."

Alison shrugged, smiled and took the videotape from her assistant as though it were as fragile and valuable as a Fabergé egg. She put it in her soft-sided briefcase with feigned casualness, trying not to let on how important it was to her. She didn't want even Dee to know the terrible deed she was about to commit.

She thanked Dee and left the office, her legs shaking as she opened her car door. It wasn't a long drive to Highland Park, but on the way she went over every horrible detail about Felicity she could think of, from the commercials she had flubbed to the silk blouses she had puked on. That last detail especially ought to make Mrs. Van Hoffelmeyer-Burnstead think twice about her adoption options.

She half expected lightning to strike her Toyota at any moment and hoped her evil deed wouldn't sap what good karma she had. She definitely wanted to be a good role model for Felicity when she adopted her. But how was that ever going to happen if she didn't prevent this horrible couple from taking her baby from her? Besides, she rationalized, if these people were so put off by a videotape of a wailing child and a few vomit stories, then they didn't deserve Felicity.

Her heart beat faster when she swung onto Mockingbird Lane, which took her closer and closer to the ritzy section of town. *Stay calm.* If she let the couple see what she was up to, how valuable Felicity was to her, everything would blow up in her face. Of course, she'd done a pretty cool job of pulling the wool over Sister Joan's eyes.

Five minutes later she was on the street. Beverly. Actually it was more like an avenue or even a boulevard. On either side of the street, huge green lawns, clipped and landscaped to perfection, unfurled lazily up to large houses, most of them two stories and made of brick or stone. The yards alone took up more space than her entire apartment complex did. And the garages looked more luxurious than any of the places she'd lived in.

Alison slowed her car as she watched the numbered addresses. As she came closer to her destination, doubt surged through her. Maybe Felicity *would* be happier here, she thought. What kid wouldn't want to grow up with a huge lawn, in a safe neighborhood with the best schools, and sidewalks to play hopscotch on, and servants at her beck and call?

Her plan, which seemed so sturdy just seconds before, began to crumble. What if she met the Van Hoffelmeyer-Burnsteads and discovered that they really *were* nice people? That they just wanted to make sure they and Felicity were a good match? That was reasonable, wasn't it?

She would have to play it by ear, she thought glumly. The videotape would stay in her briefcase until she was certain they were as horrible as she sincerely hoped they were.

She reached the house that corresponded with the number on the paper Sister Joan had given her and got out of her car. When she looked up at the two-story house, though, she felt even glummer. The place looked perfect. Just the kind of home a kid would love to grow up in. She could almost see children playing in the yard…

With a couple of golden-retriever puppies.

Alison froze as Dee's phrase from earlier in the day echoed through her head. Then her breath caught in her throat. This was *that* house—the one whose picture someone had been faxing to her all week!

What the hell was going on?

She clutched her briefcase close to her chest and approached the front door suspiciously. Had the Van

Hoffelmeyer-Burnsteads been sending her pictures of their house? And why? The place, which was made of stone with wood eaves, looked even more beautiful in 3-D. Huge elms shaded the property, giving it a charming inviting look. There was even a pleasant smoky smell coming from somewhere nearby, making her think of outdoor family barbecues. But if they'd been trying to assure her in advance that they had a nice home to raise Felicity in, they should have sent along some kind of note.

When she reached the front door with its huge brass knocker, she felt instinctively that her chances of convincing the family they didn't want Felicity were small. Maybe, instead, she should be truthful and try to convince them of how much Felicity meant to *her*. She knew she couldn't compete with all their money.

She frowned and tore off a note that had been taped to the door. It had her name on it and read, "We're out back."

Hmm. That was strange.

In about the fifth time in as many minutes, Alison changed her mind completely about the Van Hoffelmeyer-Burnsteads. They might just be a bit on the loony side. In which case, perhaps she should have brought a video camera to make a tape of *them* to take back to St. Felicity's.

Feeling a bit more confident, she marched down the manicured sidewalk lined with pansies to the back iron gate.

At her first glimpse of the backyard, she gasped in surprise. The afternoon light was beginning to wane, but the flagstone path winding through the lush green yard was lined with lighted torches. She carefully followed the path, feeling more than a little wary, like

Dorothy taking the Yellow Brick Road out of the land of the Munchkins. An ample swimming pool was lined with sand, giving the sense of a beach. It was a clever effect. She wondered if the family was about to have some kind of party.

And where was everybody?

As if in answer to her question, a familiar gurgly squeak and the sound of small hands clapping came from nearby. Alison pivoted, and when she saw Felicity, her heart stopped. The baby was perched on the back porch of the house, surrounded by pineapples and coconuts, wearing nothing but a lei, a grass skirt and a diaper. She reached out to Alison, and with an instinctive burst of love, Alison hurried over and gathered the baby to her in an exuberant hug.

"What's happening, sweetie?" she asked Felicity, kissing her soft curls. "And where did you get your new outfit?"

Felicity answered her with a jumble of different sounds, all happy. In spite of being completely confused and still a little apprehensive that the Van Hoffelmeyer-Burnsteads were watching somewhere nearby, Alison laughed. "Oh, I see," she said to Felicity, giving her a nibbly kiss on her ear that made her burst into a peal of merry babbling. "Thank you for clearing that up for me."

"Don't you think we should clear *everything* up now?"

At the sound of the familiar deep voice, Alison looked up and saw Ross leaning against the now opened door behind Felicity. His rusty hair looked almost brown in the light, but his eyes glinted with their usual humor. In his hand was a bright orange frozen drink with a little rice-paper umbrella stuck in it. She gasped in surprise.

"You!" she said. She was relieved and thrilled—and confused.

"What are you doing here?"

He gestured to the backyard and house. "You mean in our home?"

Hugging Felicity to her breast, she jumped up. "*Our* home?"

He grinned. "I thought maybe after two weeks back you might be ready for an impromptu honeymoon."

Behind him, she could hear the soothing croon of Don Ho lilting through the house. Understanding struck her with the force of a blow. Her dream honeymoon in Hawaii—he was giving it to her.

"Until I met you, Alison, I thought I had everything in control," Ross said. "But since storming into your office, I haven't handled anything right. Not my dad, and certainly not my feelings for you."

"Oh, Ross..."

She was ready to fall into his arms, but he held up a hand. "I should have told you back at the cabin how much you meant to me—how much I loved you. I should never have let you get away from me."

He *loved* her? Alison's eyes welled with tears of joy. "Oh, Ross, I've been eating my heart out since we've been apart. I'm so in love with you...and I thought you didn't care at all."

"Care? I've cared from the first moment I knew you—even when you were a nun! I kept expecting to be struck by lightning. I didn't expect to be struck by love."

His words melted her every doubt. He hadn't abandoned her and Felicity; he'd only been giving her room to think—and to make up her mind. Boy, was it made up! She rushed toward him, and in a moment the three of them were locked in a tight embrace that the world's largest crowbar couldn't have pried apart. Ross bent down and kissed Alison on the lips, tentatively at first, showing her that, for all the cocksuredness his Hawaiian-themed reunion had presented, he hadn't taken her reaction for granted.

She savored the kiss until she felt Felicity squirm impatiently in her arms. "Oh, Ross—I was so wrong."

"No, *I* was wrong to expect you to just rush into everything," Ross said.

"But I want to rush now. I want…" She tore her gaze away from his dazzling blue eyes and looked around the yard. "Is this place really ours?"

"With your approval, we close on it next week," he said. "I had to get special permission to use it tonight. The Realtor thinks I'm nuts, by the way."

She laughed, thinking of all the trouble he must have gone to—and how strange the current owners must have thought him when he told them he wanted to throw a surprise luau for his wife. Then, an even happier thought occurred to her. "Then the Van Hoffelmeyer-Burnsteads don't exist?"

He shook his head, causing Alison to heave a big sigh of relief. "Except in Sister Joan's devious imagination."

Alison remembered the cool way the nun had lied to her and was amazed. "She really had me convinced! I was supposed to come here and…" She felt a blush heat her face when she remembered what she'd actually *intended* to tell the nonexistent couple about Felicity.

"Were you really going to let them adopt our baby out from under us?" he asked.

She gestured at her briefcase. "No. Actually I was going to show them a video of two hours' worth of Felicity's temper tantrums."

He bent down and gave Alison a kiss. "Good thinking, sweetie-bunch." He told her that he had approached Sister Catherine herself about adopting Felicity, and the nun had been eager to set the legal gears in motion; she did warn Ross, however, that he should hire a professional gardener.

It was all so incredible. Minutes before, Alison had been wondering if she would ever be able to have Felicity—now she discovered that she'd had every bit of happiness she had ever dared hope for dropped in her lap. "I can't believe how wonderful you are," she whispered, thanking him with a kiss. "But what about your dad? And my mom! Thank heavens we didn't tell them the truth!"

Ross made an *ahem* noise in his throat, raising an alarm. "Actually, I didn't have to tell them. They figured it out for themselves."

Alison's eyes widened in alarm. "Oh, no," she breathed.

"It's okay," he assured her. "They forgive us."

She looked at him doubtfully.

"You can ask them for yourself," he told her, nodding his head toward the kitchen.

She looked beyond him to the room inside and saw Henry and Babs peeking around a door. "You don't mind if you have company for the first half of your reunion, do you?" Henry asked.

Alison laughed, then ran over to give him a hug. Forgiveness was a blessing. Of course she was sure his granddaughter had more than a little to do with Henry's amiability.

"The more the merrier," she said, greeting her mother with a hug, too.

Babs was all enthusiasm. "My dear, this house is a dream—and what an address! I always knew my little girl would land in the best part of town. You've *got* to get a load of this library. Oak paneling! And beautiful marble in the hallway! What taste!"

Alison smiled helplessly at Ross.

"I've been trying to convince Henry to get a little pied-à-terre nearby so that he can visit his grandbaby," Babs went on. Then she looked at him and winked, adding, "And the rest of us."

Ross and Alison exchanged suspicious glances. Henry and Babs? Alison had expected her mother to be happy for her sake, but she'd forgotten that Babs might still be looking for a love of her own. She was amazed and a little pleased by the idea. After all, who was she to question love? She certainly had it sneak up on herself when she'd least expected it.

Ross pulled her to him and escorted her outside again while the grandparents were distracted by Felicity's antics.

"Don't get me wrong," he told her. "I intend to take you to Hawaii for real someday soon. Just like you've always wanted." His mouth quirked wryly. "We'll get that cozy little bungalow, too."

She laughed. "Dreams can become infectious, I guess."

He pulled her close and nibbled softly and seductively at her ear.

"If you've got any other dreams as good as this one," he whispered, "infect away."

Feeling as if her world lacked only one thing to be perfectly complete, she lifted her lips to his and kissed him.

COMING NEXT MONTH

#769 SUDDENLY A DADDY by Mindy Neff
Delaney's Grooms
Dylan Montgomery was the kind of man who could take anything on the chin. But when Dylan found one of Karl Delaney's infamous notes in his coat pocket that said he would be a daddy, a light breeze could have flattened Dylan. Because the only mommy could be...Karl's niece, Whitney Emerson.

#770 THE HUNK & THE VIRGIN by Muriel Jensen
Being stuck with gorgeous stud Gib London for six weeks was going to be torture for old-fashioned Kathy McQuade. The sexy bodyguard was supposed to be guarding her virtue—not tempting her to abandon it!

#771 THE MOST ELIGIBLE...DADDY by Tina Leonard
Sexy Single Dads
Noreen Cartwright's elderly relatives were on a mission: to get her off the shelf. Since the stubborn young woman wanted no time with a fella, the three ladies set to matchmaking her with Parker Walden—the sexiest man and most eligible daddy Rockwall, Texas, had ever seen!

#772 HOW TO CATCH A COWBOY by Karen Toller Whittenburg
Kurt McCauley had long been a thorn in Emily Dawson's side. But while the too-handsome, too-famous cowboy was pining for Emily's sister, he somehow wound up married to Emily! They'd just have to get an annulment—except, Kurt knew they'd had a wedding night. And might be having a baby...